Finale

Published by Raw Dog Screaming Press
Hyattsville, MD

First Edition

Cover Design: M. Garrow Bourke
Book Design: Jennifer Barnes

Printed in the United States of America

ISBN 978-1-933293-84-4

Library of Congress Control Number: 2009927603

www.RawDogScreaming.com

Finale

by Paul Toth

RAW DOG
SCREAMING
PRESS

Other Novels by Paul A. Toth

For Michael Grossklaus

Table of Contents

Eight

Divided I crawled, semi-united I stood, and disembodied I fell. All I ever wanted was to walk the line like Johnny Cash, strong and true, but the line walked me until that letter arrived, and then it stomped me. It might be said it wasn't even a line but a circle or a hole.

I ran my fingernail along the words, pressed deep into the paper by what must have been more punching than typing.

> "If I were you, I'd keep your potatoes peeled. Make sure they don't get mashed. Maybe then you'll keep your eyes on one girl. Or maybe you won't stay in one place until you're dead."
>
> Love,
>
> M.W.

M.W.: Mary Whitcomb, a menthol cigarette, cool on top, sweet underneath, tar deep inside. She liked to burrow into my armpit and sleep until noon. She didn't saw logs; she clearcut the rainforest. "You've got weird eyes," she often said, "like you'd have to hang upside down to cry." She was somebody I tried to forget. But when the envelope arrived postmarked San Diego, California, I knew it had to be from Mary Whitcomb.

I thought about playing pepper off Rosie's brain about the letter, but I'd been getting bored before it ever arrived. Rosie knew it, too. For months, I'd been daydreaming about the women in my past. And when Rosie phoned my unnatural mother from behind the bedroom door, I knew they were talking about the resurrection of The Wanderer.

I'd been in one place for two years. Long before, prior to the closing of the General Motors' plant in Saginaw, Michigan, I took a buyout. They offered me a pension plus free room and board at vacation resorts across the nation. I knew that plant was headed to Mexico, so I grabbed the deal. I was ready to begin the wandering Mother so hated, blaming it on herself, I suppose. I went straight to California and never left.

For years, I found my way to every kind of golden place and woman, including San Diego and Mary Whitcomb. At the end of my wandering, I met Rosie, a black cloud blocking the sun. I enjoyed her on my semi-white chest, holding me down. Mother liked Rosie. Though Mother was no friend to minorities, I had finally ceased being The Wanderer, as she had named me during the post-factory years.

Rosie and I lived in a canyon house three hours from San Francisco, where the only sound came from trucks on the way north and south. I paid for it with my resort deal, selling it to another guy retiring young. It was like selling it to myself, only I thought I'd changed. There was a day I would have tattooed Rosie on my chest, like my namesake song said. But the time was coming when I might have wanted that name sandblasted off my skin.

Our house was so far from civilization that the nearest paper, *The Gooseberry Daily Sentinel*, took two days to arrive by mail. What that sentinel was on the lookout for was anybody's guess because nothing ever happened. But Rosie insisted, "Educated motherfuckers read the newspaper," and so the papers piled unread beside the couch.

I folded the letter and slipped it into my shirt pocket. I was already thinking about taking a trip to San Diego and knocking on Mary Whitcomb's door. Although I wasn't planning on leaving for good, I couldn't be sure I was coming back. Rosie was eating more and more and lately eyeing me. I kept a full fridge, and I wasn't planning on jumping inside.

She was pulling dirty tricks, trying to voodoo me into staying put, one day teasing me with lingerie, the next pretending to ignore me, reading her books. Sometimes she wailed and hollered, other times she knelt beside the bed and prayed. "Goddamn it," she'd whisper, "change him, Lord."

Now she emerged from the bedroom draped in slink, the negligee colorizing those big brown nipples red as Mars, her heart full of war.

"What the hell'd you just stick in your pocket?"

I shrugged, knowing she'd been watching behind my back. "Nothing."

"I can see the goddamn paper from here. What is it, a love letter?"

She stood in front of a bookshelf that bowed under the weight of works by Zora Neale Hurston, Toni Morrison, Maya Angelou, Alice Walker. On a stand in the center was the prized first edition of Harriet Beecher Stowe's *Uncle Tom's Cabin*. "This is my cabin," Rosie liked to say, "and you're my Uncle Tom."

"But Rosie," I'd say, "I'm not black."

"Well, you live like a black man. Probably die when you're forty."

"I'm already forty."

"Then you already dead."

We played that scene a hundred times, a one-act play for visitors who never arrived.

The trouble with Rosie? I could never be sure which version was more real than the other, the Rosie who mocked and derided me or the Rosie with whom I shared a love of self-mis-education.

For me, it started at the factory. I had to keep my head full to sit there pulling a lever all day. When I wasn't at work, I read, went to museums and libraries, bought all the records I could, just to keep my mind on something besides the clock and the machine. Sometimes I thought I'd give writing a try, but when I went to a bookstore and browsed the new releases, I found that modern literature concerned itself and nobody else with domestic minutiae, divorce its favorite subject, usually between two professors, a world without a sky, populated by those whose educations had consumed them, leaving no choice but to do the suburban waltz, their only relief dogs and nostalgia for baseball, their only hope the nose-chained children they had botched and now put the weight of the future upon, for that was their mantra: "The children, the children!" A whodunit or blastoff to Mars had more relevance and reality than these tales of comfortable woe. But one day I would find a trajectory for my imagination, perhaps this very journey.

Rosie, on the other hand, read to recreate herself, everything she learned reshuffled into a Rosie-poped Vatican complete with its own cathedral. She believed Jesus was a holy ghost, but she didn't believe he was a god. She said he sometimes interposed on our behalf, depending on his mood. She insisted cursing in prayer was appropriate, for it attracted his attention. And so it was not uncommon to hear her in the kitchen yelling, "Motherfuck it, Lord, just once make this man do the goddamn dishes."

Her breasts pinched the gold crucifix as she bent toward me and snatched the envelope from my pocket.

"Son of a bitch," she said, scanning the note fast. "What the hell is it?"

"It's a letter."

"I can see that, Tom. Who the fuck's it from?"

"I got a feeling—"

"You got a feeling what?"

"It's from a girl I used to know."

"White girl? Well, what's it for? You get some girl pregnant?"

"I don't know what it's for, but I'm thinking about finding out."

"You are, huh? I'll get the road atlas."

12

Unbeknownst to me, the atlas had for some time slept beneath the bookshelf, waiting for a honeymoon trip we'd never taken. She tossed it at me.

"There you go."

"Rosie, I—"

"Rosie you what? You thinking about going? Go."

"Let me think, would you? It's a threat, not a love letter."

Outside, trucks zoomed past. Her nipples stared at me, the two red planets glowing with impending violence. Sometimes I shivered when alone with her. It wasn't hard to imagine Jesus slipping her a knife when the mood was right, like right now.

My head ached with wanderlust and fear. I was too bored to stay, too afraid to leave. I'd never been good at being alone, starting with my youngest years, when Mother would toss a soccer ball at my feet and yell, "Kick it! Anybody can play soccer. Kick it like a boy, goddamn it!"

I'd only slept with ten women, Rosie included. I didn't lose my virginity until I was twenty years old. When relationships ended, I moved. My lengthiest stint in one place was that factory, and I lived those years by myself, too crazy from pulling a lever ten hours a day for anyone to bear afterwards. I felt up a few women now and then, but I couldn't get under their skin the way I liked. They left before they came.

On the road, my modus operandi was to meet a woman by chance and start talking. I was a wayward cat, and it surprised me how often I found myself in a new owner's home within hours, more adoptee than lover. Each guardian soon learned why I shuffled from home to home. But still the next would accept me, first with a bowl of milk, then an open door, and finally the bed. Luckily, this kitten had a wallet in his paw, filled with pension checks.

Why the hell would Mary Whitcomb write me now, so many years after we split? And if Rosie couldn't hold me down, who could?

Finale

"What you rubbing your head for?" she said. "You ain't thinking. You already decided."

She traipsed past me to the bedroom and left the door open. She was right: I'd already decided. I opened the atlas and traced a line to San Diego.

"Get in here," she called from the bedroom. "You ain't leaving without giving me some sex."

A few seconds later, she pancaked me. She came down in every direction, mountains of skin overlooking the sunlit valley below. She wrapped that nightgown around my wrists, and before I could escape, she had me tied me to the bedpost.

"Where you going *now*?"

With all her shrieking and bellowing, I was glad we had no neighbors.

"Bring it, Jesus, bring it."

It was a geometry problem gone awry, a hundred shapes of flesh, blobs that hung in the air, cellulite satellites. All the while I was thinking about what I should pack, why I was going, and what would happen when I arrived.

"What the hell you ruminating about?" she said, slapping my jaw like an irate mother at the shopping mall.

"Sorry."

Usually with Rosie, I got so far into her that I practically became her, wondering more what it felt like to be her than worried about my own pleasure. I had a second sense that way, and my girlfriends always told me I wasn't like other guys when it came to sex. To me, it was intuition, but that was lost on me now. For all her flailing, Rosie might as well have been alone. I had allowed myself to be taken outside of her, a patient on a stretcher rolled into an ambulance, only I suspected the ambulance wasn't going to the hospital; maybe the mental institute. Somehow, I was driving at the same time I rode in back.

She rolled off, not bothering to untie me. "Fuck it, I'm done."

14

"You think," I said, "you might let me loose?"

"Oh, I'm cutting you loose, Tom. I might be here when you get back, might not. Don't worry, I'll leave the fake wood paneling and your shag rug carpet and your piece of shit TV and your goddamn laptop computer. All I need's my books."

"Maybe you should have married a black guy, Rosie. Culturally, I mean."

"What'd I just get done telling you not five minutes ago, Uncle Tom?"

"Listen, I'm white as an albino."

"Al who? Those books tell me about myself. They got nothing to do with you."

"Come on," I said, "untie me."

"Only if you kneel down and pray with me."

"You know I don't pray."

"Then you better start. Get down on your knees like a good boy, else I'll call your mother."

She undid the tent that bound me to the bedposts and pulled it over her head, staking two corners on her breasts and the other two on her double-wide ankles. We spun off the bed and knelt.

"Goddamn it, Jesus, you bring this dumb motherfucker back better than he left. I don't got much more time in life to waste on this stupid son of a bitch, so if you give a good goddamn what happens to old Rosie, you better set to action, Lord."

My hands were crossed, but even as a stalwart agnostic, I was afraid to finish that prayer.

"Well?" she said.

"Amen," I mumbled.

"Goddamn right, amen. Now get your ass out of here. I want the whole bed tonight. I'm gonna sleep you off, and when I wake up, you better be gone. Don't come back 'til you're done being a private dick."

Finale

She left. She said more prayers. I turned on my piece of shit TV, *The Postman Always Rings Twice* on channel 52. The black and white cooled me, flecks and ticks of debris floating across the screen. I still smelled like Rosie. Let's just say Rosie didn't smell like roses after a good round in the ring. With all that grabbing and holding, and no referee to step between and separate us, bodily fluids had a way of trading places.

Meanwhile, I was having private dick thoughts about that letter and second thoughts about the whole idea of leaving. The movie wasn't helping. I guess the crew at Channel 52 would have had a good laugh if they knew I was watching their programming right then. They probably had a guy in my backyard with a stethoscope against the house. He'd phone the studio and say, "You're not gonna believe this, but there's this guy out here in the middle of nowhere who—never mind. Just keep running *The Postman Always Rings Twice*. I'll explain later. You're gonna shit yourself when I tell ya."

It was no crazier than Mary Whitcomb sending me a letter across all that space and time, brushing off the black hair that fell on the envelope when she sealed it. She had the flapper girl hairchop down and never did she change that style. She would smoke herself to death trying to look like she belonged in movies, and if they wheeled in a camera to film her demise from emphysema, she would Louise Brook no regrets. But when nobody was looking, she'd pull out her supply of stuffed animals, the bears and tigers fluffed with love, and squeeze them tight, snoring through an extra supply of phlegm.

Oh, Christ, why I was going? Was I having a spell? It felt like one, like I'd been mesmerized. No point in lying about it. I was already thinking of laying Mary Whitcomb across the bed like a sheet of rolling paper and wrapping myself inside. I'd be her tobacco, laced with all the poison inside me. And if Rosie stayed behind, I bet Jesus would be at her side when I returned, armed with two by fours and nails.

I'd take my laptop computer. Late at night, I sometimes looked up those

16

other women. They were all still located right where they'd been when I left them. And if they did move, I knew from junk e-mail that real private dicks could find "anybody, anywhere, for $29.95." Because for all I knew, somebody was playing a trick on me through Mary Whitcomb, using her to lure me into a trap.

As I fell asleep on the couch, the cloud of Rosie rose above while the exhaust from the factory I'd left behind spiraled toward me in a thousand-mile wisp, even though the factory wasn't there anymore. A song played over and over again in my head: "Oh, Rosie. Oooooh, Rooooooooosie. Steal away now, now, steal away." I imagined that factory splitting down the middle, forming a bullethole-shaped vagina that spat me out. And the post-man hadn't even bothered ringing once before delivering that envelope.

"Get up, bitch."

There must have been eighteen eggs cooking on the stove, two for me, plus one of the three stacks of waffles and two of the eight sausage links. It was a rare morning our home didn't smell like The International House of Pancakes, but I wasn't expecting breakfast today. In fact, I had planned on being gone by then.

"Got to eat, Tom."

Life with Rosie had imparted a taste for food I hadn't always possessed. I weighed 150 when we met and 200 now. Sideways, I looked like a pregnant anorexic, my legs still skinny but topped by a beach ball. I'd already planned on resuming smoking after I left. I'd need something to do on the road, and the nicotine would cut my food expense.

"Get your ass to the kitchen table," she said. "Might as well stuff your fat face one last time."

I bowed for the blessing.

"Thank you, Lord, for this food, which we all know this lazy motherfucker is lucky to provide. We acknowledge the luck comes from you, not him. How he ever got lucky twice, once with money and once with me, is beyond the both of us, Jesus. Amen."

As usual, I crossed myself like a kid trying to sign his name for the first time. I wasn't being sacrilegious; I didn't want to sign off on Rosie's religion, just in case.

"Here's what you think of me, you goddamn racist," she said, squeezing the Aunt Jemima bottle until a lake of syrup flooded her plate. "I ain't your damn aunt. But you're still Uncle Tom."

"Knock it off with that, would you?"

She reached across the table and tried to smack me, but for once I backed away in time.

"Shut your ass and eat."

Despite appearances, Rosie was not earthy. Sometimes I thought she ate to weigh herself down, so spacey was she with her weird conceptions. Mother considered Rosie well-grounded, and I suppose like a wide-bodied jet on the tarmac, she was. But she was even more than met the eye. She soaked up books and made them into something new, every word supporting not the author's intent but Rosie's self-design. Each year, the slaps came harder. Each year, she was more in charge, until she finally handled all the finances, keeping the investments in line and telling me what I could spend on what. The accounts might be joint, but Rosie was the tendon, the muscle.

Finally, I said what I had originally intended to skip. "I got to go to the bank."

"It's your money."

"That's not what you usually say."

"That's what I'm saying now." She stuck her fork in the stack of waffles. It stood straight, a reed in Lake Syrup. "You do what you gotta do. Rosie will survive. You think I didn't open up my own account, just in case? I got plenty. You can't surprise me. I knew you'd pull something sooner or later. If you don't come back, I can always get a job cooking down at the truck stop. You know I can cook. Men in truck stops get lonely, and there's plenty of men as smart as you down there. Or maybe I'll just take a break from cooking at home, now that I think of it, and take myself out to eat every now and then. Can't say what I'll do while you're gone. That's my business, just like you got your business."

The thought of some guy hanging his NASCAR cap on my bedpost gave me yet another second thought. But this was all happening so easily, Rosie just letting me go, that it seemed I was meant to leave. It was now or never.

I wiped my mouth clean of syrup and crumbs and went to the bedroom. I found my old luggage bag in the closet and packed all the clothes I could fit. I strapped the laptop to my shoulder. I washed up in the bathroom and packed my razors; if and when I came back, the sink would be clean of another man's beard.

I was leaving before the mail would arrive. If Mary Whitcomb had sent a second letter, after sobering up and remembering what she'd written the night before, I'd never receive it.

Rosie met me at the door.

"I loves you, Bess," she said.

"You got it mixed up, Rosie. I'd be Porgy, the crippled one. Why you always trying to make a fool of me? You know I'm a guy."

"Mmm."

She laid a French kiss on me, a melting Eiffel Tower down my throat.

"Well," she said, "goodbye."

"Bye, Rosie."

After I threw the suitcase and laptop in the back seat and climbed behind the steering wheel, I planned to wave goodbye, but the door was already closed. I started to cry. Maybe Miles Davis should have played *I Loves You,*

Finale

Porgy. Since he couldn't make it, I turned on the radio. All I could find was the country music those boys at the truck stop favored.

The one thing Rosie never made for breakfast was coffee. Coffee's a business drink. Rosie and I had no business other than biding time, so coffee was a rarity. Yet there I was not three miles from home when all that food started making me sleepy, my mind slow as syrup in the early morning haze.

There was one stop before the highway: Rosie's future love nest, the Giant Travel Plaza, which served as liquor mart, gas station, restaurant, grocery store and condom dispenser for a hundred mile radius. I bet everybody in that circle had their Giant route memorized, every tree, every bump in the road. I was no different, and it wasn't hard finding my way even with half-closed eyes.

Soon the waitress led me to the usual orange vinyl booth.

"Just coffee."

"Yuh," she replied, as if I wasn't worth the expenditure of a single actual word.

I must have sat there for an hour, drinking one cup after the next. Between cups, I went to the register and bought my first pack of cigarettes in years. Then I sat down and unwound the wrapper, a habit still so familiar it was tantamount to time travel. The nicotine high surprised me. By the time I'd quit, cigarettes were as intoxicating as oxygen, but now it electrified me. Soon, I was dizzy with the caffeine-nicotine buzz and feeling confused.

I sat there holding my head and watching the other customers, truckers mostly, all in baseball caps and none looking too thrilled to exist. I knew they lived a hard life, but I could offer no sympathy if their only succor would come in the form of Rosie. The thought irritated me, my skin percolating.

A likely candidate sat facing me in the next booth. He was Rosie's kind of guy, skinnier than me when we'd met, lean as quality pork. Every now and then he caught my stare. I could read his lips: "Whatchoo lookin' at?" And then he said exactly that.

"Not looking at anything."

"That supposed to mean something?"

"Just drinking coffee."

"Then drink it and look at something else."

I tried but couldn't. If there's one sure way to make my brain go down a road, it's to erect a bright red "WRONG WAY" sign. And so my eyes kept trailing back to him. Suddenly, he seemed to occupy my bed, Rosie bouncing up and down, telling him how good it was to have a skinny white guy underneath her again. She'd probably say, "I thank the hell out you, Jesus. It's been a long time."

He'd get breakfast in the morning and watch my TV. He might fancy the fake wood paneling, a hell of a lot more pleasant surroundings than a truck cab. He'd kick his feet up on the couch and switch through the channels with my remote control. Then he and Rosie would go for seconds, and I don't mean eggs and toast.

Suddenly, I was staring at a Led Zeppelin belt buckle.

"What'd I just tell you?"

I'm a little short when it comes to testosterone. I felt the need to be honest, to resolve this mess before it spilled in every direction. "I'm just worried about my wife, that's all."

"What's your wife's name, pal?"

"Rosie."

"Well, then, let me ease your mind: Rosie ain't the name of the somebody-else's wife I'm sleeping with. Now quit staring at me."

He went back to his booth.

"It's not just that," I said, loud enough for everyone in the joint to hear.

21

Finale

"I don't want any man in this place thinking funny thoughts about my wife. She's a vulnerable woman."

Now they all stared at me. I heard the mumbles but not the words. I could guess. I grabbed my cigarettes. I left five dollars on the table and received not so much as a nod of thanks from the waitress.

At the register, a new cashier, young girl with porcupine hair—if porcupines dyed their hair purple—said, "*Now* what?"

"One lottery ticket, numbers 0903-0903-0903."

"Ya, right, hon'."

"What's that supposed to mean?"

"It means that's a bad number. No number like that ever came up."

"It's the number I always play, my wife's birthday, September third."

"Well, blurt that out, too, so all your rivals can buy her a birthday card."

On the way out, I remembered it was the end of August. I hadn't realized that Rosie's birthday would occur in the beginning of my time away from her. In the parking lot, I dug a quarter from my pocket and dropped it in the pay phone.

"You?" she said. "You gonna leave, leave. What the fuck you want?"

"I just wanted to say," I began, but then I started crying again.

"Wanted to say what?"

"Say—happy—birthday. In advance."

"Lord Jesus fucking Christ, you crying? Don't call back 'til you been gone a while. A long while."

She hung up. I wiped my eyes with a shirt sleeve as my friend from the next booth walked past, shaking his head. I stood there a minute, and then his truck rumbled to a stop beside me.

"She must be some woman," he called down from the cab.

"Yeah," I said, "she is."

"Well," he said, tipping his cap, "good luck, buddy."

I stood in the parking lot and watched his truck pull away. He extended his arm and waved goodbye.

The sky was postcard blue with aluminum sheen. The front of the lot was lined by trucks, the back by wrecked and inoperable cars the owner must have bought at auction, fixing and selling them in the town I was going to next, Gooseberry. Green dumpsters overflowed with sun-roasted mufflers and hubcaps. The parking lot, simultaneously luminous and dull, might have been my brain turned inside out. Before I went anywhere, I had to send off these sad butterflies landing on my heart.

"Fly away, melancholy pollinators, for I am no flower."

In the car, I switched off the radio, drowning out Country Bob and the Texas Deadbeats or whoever the hell wailed away: "I took a shot of whiskey, then she took a shot at me."

That's all I needed now, to think about drinking. I didn't drink often, only when it sealed my nerve endings like glue. But afterwards, the residue bound my fingers and toes and everything else, paralyzing me. Sitting in a parking lot fading like a glossy car magazine in the sun, I could have used a bottle. But I must have blown my liver, and I could hardly afford to start this journey with a three-day hangover.

Then, as so often happens, I began to feel a little better, not *despite* the reasons for my gloom but *because* of them. I was glad Rosie answered the phone the way she had. What man would stand for her behavior? If I was Country Bob, Rosie would think twice before slapping me around. Country Bob would stagger home from The Starlight Lounge at three in the morning with lipstick on his collar and would never bother lying about its cause.

It might be said I put my cowboy hat on right about then. "To hell with Rosie."

I started the car and headed to Gooseberry, location of the bank. Only

23

Finale

that morning had it come clear to me I should have kept better track of Rosie's financial doings.

So I drove, smoking cigarettes fast as I could put them out. Every once in a while, a cloud blocked the sun. It was Rosie. I'd start feeling sleepy again and longed to rest my head on her shoulder cliff, in which the likenesses of more than four presidents might have been carved. Then the cloud passed, the day brightening. In the glare, Mary Whitcomb shimmered. I thought about her poky hipbones. I thought about her breasts, the opposite of Rosie's, nature balancing the scales. I thought about that flapper hair. And I remembered that awful painting looking down upon us, its lipstick-sunglasses-shopping-mall glamour always ruining the moment.

"It's Patrick Nagel. Nagel's famous."

"I don't care. I don't like it."

"So you're an art critic *and* retired lathe operator. I didn't know."

"I'd like to throw that piece of shit over the balcony."

"Go ahead. Don't let go."

But like I said, after a while that menthol coolness turned into something sweet, and she'd start crying.

"I love that painting," she'd whisper, sniffing. Then she'd pull herself together and say, "Go pick up my friends."

And so I'd gather the stuffed animals I'd kicked off the bed in the middle of the night.

It wasn't always that way. Long as I averted my gaze, which tended to go wherever I preferred it not, everything was lipstick and fishnet stockings. I was younger then, about the last time I was young at all. I liked black and white movies, especially late at night, and Mary seemed to fade right into the television set. The less we talked, the more she disappeared into fig-leaf figment. Unfortunately, by morning the news was on in full color. Mary transformed into a 21st century phony who might have taken the place of

24

the woman in that painting. She'd awake at noon with designs on shopping malls, where she somehow managed to find the concoctions of clothes that made her Zelda Fitzgerald the Second. I can do without the shopping mall. They give me anxiety attacks. And so do banks.

So I steeled myself like George Reeves before heading into Gooseberry National Bank, a name probably chosen to disguise the fact there was nothing national about Gooseberry; it was as local as a pothole.

When I walked inside, a long line of customers awaited me. The tellers were pretty, every one of them. I bet the manager threw their resumes in the trash and based his decision on interviews—modeling auditions, that is. I'd been in that bank a hundred times, and for as little as I knew about my finances, these tellers knew less. They should have been called non-tellers, keep-it-quieters. Yet the lines never seemed long looking at them, nor my unanswered questions so irritating when they said, "I'm sorry, Mr. Thomas, but you'll have to speak to a manager about that." Of course, there would be a shrub full of Gooseberries waiting to see that manager, and I would give up before seeing the manager every single time.

This time would be different, a simple transaction anyone could handle, even women with fingernails so long they could count my money long distance.

"What I'd like to do," I said, "is withdraw everything from my account."

"Name, sir?"

"Jonathan Thomas."

"I remember, now: John."

Yes, John Thomas, har-har. I preferred Jonathan. If in a good mood, Johnny was okay. Rosie liked Tom. Nobody ever got it right.

"Jonathan. And like I said, just withdraw everything from my account."

I gave her my account number.

"You've got three thousand dollars available."

Finale

"That's got to be a mistake. I've deposited close to three hundred thousand dollars into this bank."

Three *hundred* thousand, not three thousand. Before Rosie took over, I made a few good investments. Now Rosie handled them.

"Well," the teller said, "let me check your last few deposits...Um, the last ten deposits were made into another account, under your wife's name. But that's not a joint account. You need your wife to access that money."

"I don't need to access it, but I'd like to know what's there. You can tell me that, can't you?"

"I'm sorry. I just can't."

"Oh, damn," I said in a manner suggesting it was a word I rarely employed and usually spelled aloud to avoid swearing. "I don't know what I'll do. This is a real fix."

"I'm sorry, Mr. Thomas, but it's against our po—po—"

"Policy? I understand. It's only—well, I can't say right now. It's a personal matter. I'm sure you understand. My wife is leaving me and, frankly, I hadn't planned on it. Now rent's due and—"

"I really can't, Mr. Thomas."

She leaned toward me, motioning that I come closer.

"It's a lot," she said. "A real lot."

"Okay," I replied, satisfied with the closest I had ever come to an answer at the Gooseberry National Bank. Besides, it was Saturday, the bank closed at one o'clock, and it was ten to one. There wasn't time to dig deeper.

One minute later, I was on another pay phone.

"I'm at the bank. Now Rosie, where's all that money? All that money I made, all that money I invested?"

"Didn't I just get done telling you not to call?"

"But it's something I should know about. I thought those accounts were joint. Now you got it all tied up in your name."

26

"You're not gonna wander off and take all that money. I know you. Your mother told me all I need to know. You can bet your ass you won't be stranding me. I ain't the Titanic. I got plenty of lifeboats. If it's money you're so worried about, I'll start saving some by getting this goddamn phone shut off."

How I wanted to call a mother now as Rosie slammed the phone again. What lost boy doesn't want to hug the apron? But I couldn't phone my real mother, and the other—the one who raised me like a weed—made a poor substitute. Wasn't naming me John Thomas enough? Wasn't that when the war started, the day she took me into her home?

There was something that divided us, a deck of cards cut in two by a dealer. Maybe the dealer was a god, if there was one, or maybe it was my father choosing the Army and Vietnam—or rather, a Vietnamese woman named Sun—over the woman I called Mother. Whatever the reason, Mother and I were Pakistan and India, only there was no Kashmir at stake, just the savoring of each point we won. My victory was never phoning her, never taking her calls. Only Rosie answered, and only Rosie called. When I listened, I never detected the slightest positive conversation about me. It was always, "Your son's doing this, doing that, and then he, and then, and then he..."

I had more than enough cash for this trip, even if it took me farther than San Diego. But what if I returned home to find the locks changed, Rosie and my replacement peeking through the curtains, a hyena and her zookeeper laughing like it was the happy ending of a children's book?

And then the bad man
wandered home.
Expecting a hug,
He heard instead moans:
Rosie was not alone.

27

Finale

What pictures I painted. But I'd have to cross that bridge later, even if it opened beneath me, Rosie and the trucker waving from a boat below that left a trail of foam in its wake.

"Bye, asshole," Rosie would shout. "Thank you, Lord, with all my fucking heart!"

I drove out of Gooseberry wondering whether that letter wasn't Rosie's elaborate way of leaving me, a painless extraction. Was I a dentist's patient, gassed full of a black and white daydream Rosie had induced by somehow sending that letter herself? She knew I was a sucker for movies and probably guessed I was ripe to be sucked into one. Soon as I was gone, she'd find a new man and either take over the cabin or burn it down, leaving me to figure out the scheme when it was too late. But it was hard to believe our ties had come unbound. After all, she was the one who tied me to the bedposts.

"I loves you, Porgy," she'd said, and "love" was a word Rosie rarely mentioned. I guess I liked her pushing me around at the same time I despised it. I was a guy in a wheelchair, hating his situation but occasionally enjoying the ride and even the resentment of the person providing it.

I was getting paranoid. My mind works in terms of story, but the world doesn't. The world never says "The End" but keeps going, the plot forever expanding, its shooting location 24,000 miles round and six feet deep. And even if I pinched a piece no bigger than the space between my thumb and finger, seen through a microscope it was one hundred times as big and complicated. Some people narrowed and confined the plot. I tried but couldn't do it. Everything seemed equally possible, perhaps even equally true.

Rosie kept me snapped in place, and I was a crucial Lincoln Log in our cabin. Maybe with me gone, she'd find the roof leaked.

"Rosie isn't going anywhere," I told myself, trying to calm my imagination.

That night, I slept in a little motel right off the highway. I've always liked hotels, mansions for travelers complete with maids and a butler at the desk. Motels are temporary ghettos complete with all the grime and dust of home. I would have slept in hotel, but I couldn't with the money in my wallet, not before I knew how long my trip would last. Rosie had made this bed, and now I was sleeping in it. I was glad I had no microscope.

I climbed under the sheets, and for the first time in years I had more room than I needed. Without Rosie, bed was a first class cabin, unoccupied. Usually I slept with my back to her and had to rest one arm over the side of the mattress, maintaining a gymnast's awareness of gravity. Sometimes she rolled over and knocked me off my balancing beam. I'd head to the couch in the diaspora of the sleepless. But now the bed felt like that couch, a lonely, nation-less place. Like a retired Olympic gymnast, I had no idea what to do with myself.

I looked at the phone. I knew better than to call Rosie. If I woke her, she would howl with the rage of Job:

> *Climbin' up d' mountain, children,*
> *Didn't come here to stay.*
> *And if I nevermore see Tom again,*
> *Gonna meet him at de judgment day.*
> *John Thomas in de fiery furnace,*
> *And dey begin to pray.*
> *And de good Lawd let dat fire roar.*
> *Oh, wasn't dat a mighty day!*
> *Goddamn it, Lord, wasn't dat a mighty day!*
> *Uncle went in de lions den,*
> *And he begin to pray.*
> *And de angels of de Lawd opened de lion's jaw.*

Finale

Oh, wasn't dat a mighty day!
Goddamn it, Lord, wasn't dat a mighty day!

I knew those reinvented lyrics well; I'd heard her sing them a hundred times.

So I became my own drill sergeant, a skill learned in the factory. When the industrial sounds of that black mass under metal skies drew me into its voodoo rhythm, I'd tell myself, "March on, Private, march on, lest you want to feel this boot in your ass." And if that failed, I would bend my mind like a spoon, using all my powers to recall a poem I had memorized from a book at home:

Ye rigid Plowmen! Bear in mind
Your labor is for future hours.
Advance! spare not! nor look behind!
Plow deep and straight with all your powers!

I remembered all of those exercises as I battled my desire to call Rosie. I also remembered how I had thought my troubles would be over once I left the factory. Probably everybody dreams of the sunny river down which they'll merrily float once their adolescent siren songs subside. Then they dream of a riverboat upon which they'll marry, drifting in a lagoon. Next, they picture a quiet raft, with no room for spouses, which takes them over rapids back to quiet waters. Finally, they imagine the anchored ship of their retirement, with no challenge aboard greater than shuffleboard. They keep dreaming of that river until the day they die, because no matter how far they travel or how much they suffer, it stays miles ahead, as if fleeing their arrival.

Should I? I did. Not Rosie; "Mother." She was still in Michigan, way up north, where she'd fled after my father left. She lived in a town with a liquor store and a church. That's all she needed, a church for repentant

30

Sunday mornings and a liquor store for seven nights a week. She would still be awake, thanks to the time difference. So I dialed.

"Hello?" she said, only it was more like, "Hemmo?" She was drunk, of course. I knew because I had called after sundown, Michigan time, a starting gun she obeyed with such dedication that in summer months she forestalled the first drink until nearly ten o'clock p.m., even if she had the shakes.

For what had I called, solace? None could she offer. Mother lobbied politicians to re-invade Vietnam. She would murder the entire Vietnamese race and probably the Chinese, Japanese and Koreans, too, just for kicks. She kept the ashes of the Vietnamese flag in a golden urn.

"Hemmooooooo?"

I have slightly Asian eyes. An odd little boy. Left unnamed, to be "cared for" by Mother when Father and Sun abandoned Michigan and disappeared. Father had gone AWOL while stateside. Maybe they were in Vietnam. Maybe they were in California. I could only wonder whether Mother had driven him away, or he had driven Mother insane. But I was just another egg, and both chickens put themselves before me. They knew the answer to one riddle.

Still, sometimes I worried about this war between us. It seemed to have a secret reason underlying the one I knew, something more than I remembered and more than I cared to discover. I hoped the war was meaningless, along with the larger picture, by which I mean the world. Unlike most folks, what joy it would give me to know life had no reason or rhyme, that all was space and time, meaninglessness an open playing field. One day, I would pass through the geometry and disappear. But until then, I wished somebody would nail my feet to the floor until I was steadfast as a rock.

"Whooooo issssss thissssss?"

Was she thinking it might be Father finally come home to make amends? I could only hope so. Or did she think it was me calling to apologize? That would do. Or maybe she thought it was my real mother, Sun, calling to warn that a kung fu typhoon was on the way from the East, finally ready to kick the world clean of Mother's imperialist American aggression.

"I know who this is," she said. "Is that you—"

I hung up. Better to leave her question an unopened gift, more valuable for who gave it than what might lay inside. I cherished the wrapping, that old drunken slur of vengeance. "Sleep tight," I would have said had I been able to disguise my voice. "*Do* let the bedbugs bite."

But I'd forgotten something I remembered as soon as the phone rang: caller ID. I closed my eyes, imagining the giant fuzzy slippers she always wore when home. I heard her cursing, rifling through her book for a number that matched the motel's. Next, she'd call the operator and check the area code: California. Then she'd know. And so she knew.

The phone stopped ringing. Then it rang again. It kept ringing, ten times every ten minutes for the rest of the night.

I couldn't sleep, so I thought about my childhood. As for Sun, I've never been burdened by the ill feelings other children in my position harbor, for she wasn't meant to stay in port. Something had prevented her from mothering me, and it was best she admitted it to herself. I only wish they had left me somewhere else, in a parking lot, behind a dumpster, anywhere but with Mother.

They must have blamed part of the situation on her. From what I knew, Mother used to do plenty more than drink, and apparently the habit of speed had spread from her to Father to Sun like the flu. Or, as Mother put it in one of her post-sunset monologues, "That Chink bitch comes here clean as a whistle but now she don't think she's so bright." But things never had been too bright for Sun. From what Mother said, she had passed through the edges of a Napalm cloud before my father met her.

Father and Sun probably disappeared to cure their habits. I could imagine poor Sun, washed out from speed in the rusty Midwest, wondering why anyone dreamed of America. They might have found a place that explained it better to her, or maybe they left the States for good. I knew the Army had lost track of them along the way. They likely lived under false names somewhere. I could understand the attraction of vanishing, submerging oneself in a cover story until even reflections disappeared. But mine remained, and there was a shadow behind it.

I remembered the bedtime stories Mother used to tell me when I was little, St. John's supposed revelation further scrambled by alcohol and semi-literacy: "One day a fire's gonna burn the world clean of Chinks, Jews and Arabs. And then, my little man, you'll ride through the fire on a white horse, all the way to heaven."

Somehow, I doubt it.

The phone was still ringing the next morning. I couldn't unplug it because the jack was protected by a dresser bolted to the wall. There was no ringer control. I tried taking it off the hook, but the megaphoned orders of the operator—"If you'd like to make a call, please hang up and try again"—rang louder than the ringing. Between the ringing and the pillows over my head, I could hardly hear my neighbor shouting, "*You're* gonna ring when I shove that phone up your ass." Later: "Turn that goddamn phone *off*. Turn it off, turn it, turn it off, turn it off, turn it off, turn it *off.*"

I dressed without taking a shower. In the bathroom, I splashed water on my face, then turned off the light and left. The phone was still ringing when I closed the door.

"Why the hell," the manager said, "was that phone ringing all night long?"

His lumberjack-plaid shoulders wider than a linebacker's, I half-expected him to go outside, return with an axe the size of a redwood, raise it over my head and split me in two.

"It was my mother," I said, telling the truth only because it was less bother than inventing a lie he'd never believe.

33

Finale

"Your mother?" he said. "Your mother is a very tenacious woman."

"That's not the word I'd use."

"What word would you use?"

"Better not to say."

He looked at me: wrong answer. I dropped the room key on the counter.

"You could have left it in the room," he said. "I would have preferred it."

He was still standing there confused when I took off; he couldn't possibly imagine a mother like mine. Most sons might have been more forgiving than me, at least from a distance, but they couldn't measure my distance, nor could I explain to them why Mother's Day sentiments eluded me. There was a gulf between me and that world, a crevice, a faultline, and it was growing wider. I couldn't know that by demarcating its boundaries, I would cause an earthquake, preceded by seven minor shakers. They came at night, just before sleep, when I least expected my walls to bend.

Earthquake 1.0

My Unnatural Mother, blackened by
white trash revenge. Rosie flies the night sky
with the bear, tiger, hippopotamus.
Father departed with his secret bride.
"Lay inside her seedless, rubberized, Dad!"
Mother II dreams of smiting Vietcong,
stashing ashes in national parks.
I hear her again, God rest my childhood,
that old drunken slur, her methanol blood.
Fall asleep, de angel's boot in thy ass.
Geography calls me forward, onward.
Next, geometry, algebra, physics.
Vanish, little boy. Disappear. Run, run.
Advance! A riverboat! Shoot the Rapids!

Seven

I had been unjustly denied, but here's the thing: What I had been denied, I didn't know. I just knew I wanted it so badly that the desire became more important than its object, and that posed a danger I wouldn't understand for a long time.

Now a freeway sign indicated San Diego lay two hours ahead. I hadn't driven far enough the day before, delayed by breakfast, Giant Travel Plaza, Gooseberry National Bank and constant, fatiguing thoughts of Rosie, Mother and Mary. Anyway, it would have been too late to arrive that night on Mary's doorstep, but now it was early enough. With the outcome of my screwy genetics—the semi-Asian eyes of my wanton father and milkless adoptive mother—I feared the roll of dice and normally drove the limit. But on this occasion, I shoed the accelerator and watched the needle edge right.

I glided through Los Angeles, where I'd met Rosie. She was standing in front of me at a concert that night. I'd gone alone. All I did was ask her to sit down, please, ma'am.

"Motherfucker," she said, howling, "*you* sit down. You blocking somebody else behind you."

"I'm standing because you're standing."

"And I'm standing because the guy in front of me is standing, bitch. Why don't you listen to records at home if you wanna sit down? I think you like me, that's what I think. And if you like me, get me a beer."

That was the beginning.

Soon, Rosie took me into her home, as I had come to expect would happen. Once again, I moved from a resort with one luggage bag. Those spare, wandering years had allowed me to accumulate the wealth Rosie now controlled. Summertime was easy, the cotton high, the fish jumping...but I doubted her mama was too good looking.

Rosie spent her days singing standard religious songs. The big L.A. churches could land recording contracts for the best singers, and Rosie believed she was a caged bird. At that time, her faith was more conventional, resting on favors she believed God would grant her. In her mind, Jesus would gladly lend a back for her to step upon, and she was more than willing to test his weight-bearing capacity.

One day, I accompanied her to a meeting with Minister Acorn Jackson—yes, Acorn. Acorn was the *man* when it came to studios, more talent scout than preacher, but I liked him. He knew most singers would return after their success, depositing big contributions in the collection basket.

"Rosie," Minister Jackson said, "I'm not sure—"

"You not sure what?"

I covered my eyes. Minister Jackson was in danger of receiving the smack I knew so well.

He swallowed hard. "I'm not even sure you should be in the choir. I mean, in it, period. I've had complaints."

When Rosie accumulated anger in her cloud, I could feel the rise in barometric pressure. But Minister Jackson tapped the Bible on his desk, reminding Rosie of his station. "I'm sorry, but I'm an honest man. You probably possess some other gift. Everybody does. Yours ain't singing, though."

I would have grabbed her arms, but I was still skinny and lacked the circumference to embrace her. Instead, I touched her hand, hoping to distract her.

"Why the fuck you touching my hand? You Jesus?"

Finale

"Come on, Rosie, let's go."

"Naw."

Then she sang a spiritual I guarantee Minister Jackson had never heard before.

He covered his ears. "Please stop."

It was the birth of her four-letter sect. However low sweet chariot swung, it had never been engaged in the hit-and-run accident Rosie proposed. Meanwhile, that preacher spoke in tongues. He squirmed about his desk and dug forefingers in his ears. I pulled the back of Rosie's sweater, trying to make her sit. Instead, she spun and caught my chin with a palm flat as her notes.

"What the fuck, Rosie?"

"Fuck both you motherfuckers." She ran out of the office and into the church, screaming, "You promised me, God. I don't forget no broken promise."

That's when Jesus became for her a ghost but not a son of god. Meanwhile, Minister Jackson and I looked at each other like two orphans in a strange new house.

He said, "You gonna be all right?"

"Me? I'm used to it, Preacher. And we won't be coming back, but it was nice coming to your church. Even if I don't believe."

"Lord."

"Yes, I know."

He rubbed his forehead. "Oh, Lord."

"You could say a prayer for her."

"Sweet, sweet Lord."

"Maybe say a prayer for yourself."

"My head hurts so bad."

"At least you didn't get a slap."

"Does she—does she do that often?"

"Oh, every now and then. I never see them coming. Storm clouds behind a mountain, you might say."

"That woman would be dead if she were my—"

"Well, look at me, Preacher: I'm no match. That's probably why she picked me."

"I was wondering why she—why a skinny little white boy—I wondered. I was thinking sometimes—in the pulpit—"

"She holds me to the fire, Preacher, and more than my feet. I guess I like her pushing me around. Must be some kind of, I don't know, fetish or something."

"No, please, I'd rather not know."

"I'd better go."

"I've got to lie down."

"You lie down, Preacher."

"Yes, I must lie down."

He retreated from the office, feeling his way through the door. Rosie had scored a TKO, and I was headed for a knockout.

In the parking lot, I spotted a shoe-wide dent in the driver's door. I opened it with one hand, shielding my face with the other. I started the car. She was crying and shaking, hugging herself.

"God betrayed me, that no-good motherfucker."

"That's crazy, Rosie. Don't say that."

"What the fuck you care? You don't believe in nothing."

"Yeah, but you never know. Just to be safe, you shouldn't say that."

"Naw, naw, nobody cares about me. There ain't no God."

"Jesus, Rosie, you're gonna draw attention."

"I know Jesus still cares, but God don't. I just had an illumination."

"Revelation."

"Naw, I saw light."

Finale

"The sun's in your mirror."

"It's there for a reason. Jesus shined a light. It came from his robes. He revealed himself to me."

"Okay, okay. Let's go home."

"I hear his voice."

We drove out of that parking lot, Rosie channeling Jesus all the way home and the rest of the day. We had a little apartment in West Hollywood then, and I'm sure the neighbors must have thought we were going at it, Rosie shouting, "Lord, yes. Yes, Lord!" She needed what she was imagining right then, so I stayed quiet and out of the way.

That night in bed, it seemed the voice switched off. For the first time in hours, she spoke to me.

"I got to educate myself. Everything I believe's a goddamn lie. My mother's a lyin' bitch."

"I think parents mean well. Except my mother, but that's another—"

"She the one that told me I could sing. She probably laughing now, that crazy, drunk bitch."

"Settle down."

"She's a bitch and Father's a back-door, sneak-around, scrazzle-headed, crotch-scratching, butt-sniffing dog. And don't tell me to settle down, else I'll wallop you."

The Gospel According to Rosie, much of it written that day, in pencil, erasable when occasion necessitated. Was that why I now missed her one minute and imagined with such pleasure Mary Whitcomb's barely-covered bones the next?

San Diego appeared. For some reason, that place made me edgier than the cliffs along its beaches. It's too damn clean and clear, especially the outskirts, every house and condominium so alike their owners probably walk into next-door neighbors' homes by mistake: "What's for dinner? Oops, sorry: wrong house...again."

Mary used to live in a ground-floor apartment. According to the phone book, that's where she still lived. I remembered the way there, one of my only two homes in San Diego, counting the resort. They called it something-something Park, and the buildings faced each other like sextuplets bored with seeing the same face everywhere they looked.

As I pulled into the parking lot, what I was about to do seemed momentous and monstrous, a dangerous beginning to what I couldn't know. Adrenaline flooded my veins, fueling and revving, making me perspire with panic-sparked sweat. It was a sensation I usually avoided. When it comes to fight or flight, I'm all flight, a boxer with good legs and no fists.

But this time was different. I wanted change. I didn't know why, except perhaps that my jawline was permanently numb from Rosie's slaps, my back ached from her weight, and my gut showed the implications of our life together. Was our marriage ending? There was no way to know. But if there's one thing I'd learned in all my wandering, it's that the period preceding a breakup is often signaled by a strange sadness, as if I practiced missing someone in advance, getting used to doubting my decision before I'd even made it.

I closed the car door and moved like a private toward a battlefield. Her bedroom faced the parking lot, designed, perhaps, so that traffic would dissuade ground-floor invasions.

The window was open, the curtain billowing. Mary snored. It was noon.

"Mary," I whispered through the window. "Mary?"

"Huh? Mu-mu-ma?"

"Mary, it's me, Jonathan."

"Who?"

"Wake up, Mary."

"Goddamn it, what time is it?"

Finale

"Let me in."

"Why should I?"

The curtains peeled. She appeared, head shorn of the 1920s. She was blond now. She wasn't the same woman, the old haircut a mask. She looked harder, colder, all tar, no menthol. She wasn't happy. My journey had come to its end. Not much of a mystery.

"What in the living fuck are you doing here?"

Someone jingled behind me. I turned and saw a toolbelt. I looked up.

The semi-familiar maintenance man wasn't happy, either. "Problem?"

"No," Mary said. "It's okay, Dennis."

He studied me a moment and left. Had he recognized me?

"How'd you know I'm alone?" she said. "All right, asshole, come in, but only long enough to explain why you're here. Then go."

I went to the door and waited for the buzzer. Strange the way I remembered that noise, which left more of an impression than I'd made on Dennis the Menace. He used to come to our apartment puffing out his ring of tools as if he wore a world wrestling championship belt.

"Mary here?" he'd say.

"Air conditioning's out. So's Mary."

"Hmm. At work, I suppose. Like most hardworking, simple folk."

"I paid my debt to society, Dennis...in a factory."

This time, she didn't unlock the door and leave it open for me, as she had done when I first started visiting her years before. Instead, she made a big show of rattling the chain and jiggling the knob. By the sound of it, there were ten Mary's inside, each with one hand on the door. Maybe she was Kali now, with multiple arms and blue skin, born of anger, drinker of blood.

"This is not a movie," I whispered to myself.

The door opened not upon that painting I hated nor the pile of stuffed animals, for a lot more than Mary's haircut had changed. There was a calendar on the wall, notebooks and planners on the bed, stacks of files in the corner, books about turtles next to a computer monitor.

Now that I could see her more clearly, I realized how well I had been deceived. Without that cute little flapper cut, her true face revealed itself. If she once was bittersweet, she was only bitter now, and her past was pulled tight behind her head in a bun, nearly amputated from her skull. Meanwhile, she wore the unsexiest bathrobe ever stitched, defrizzing pink fuzz that slunk around her frame as if embarrassed to be there. I noticed in the open hall closet a line of business suits. Beside the boom box, the only object I recalled, stood not some obscure punk rock disk but one of those environmental recordings, the cover depicting a beach.

"*What?*" she said.

"You've cleaned house."

"You stink. Living in a car now? Can't take a shower? This is my office. I'm a secretary. Executive secretary."

"Never mind that," I said. "What about this?"

I handed her the envelope. As she reached for it, I realized she could have torn it into pieces and let the evidence drizzle on the carpet. But she didn't. She read and gave it back.

"I don't have a typewriter."

"You could borrow one."

"From who, Hemingway? Anybody could have sent this. It wasn't me."

She waited. I wasn't sure what to say.

"You mean—" She interrupted herself, laughing. "You mean to say you think I obsess about you? That I'm stalking you? Actually, you know what: You're right. I've been missing you *so much* all these years. Thank God you've come home, Bill Bailey. 'Mashed potatoes.' Are you kidding me? You know what I think? I think you wrote this. You're the manual typewriter type."

"Well, somebody sent it, unless you think I put a U.S. Postal Service uniform on and delivered it to myself. So sit down. Let's think about this."

Besides the bed, the only furniture was the computer desk and two director-style chairs. I could see the tiny room in back, supposedly meant for a bed and where she had once stored her more valuable stuffed animals. Obviously, she had outgrown her friends. I wondered who or what had replaced them.

"You've really changed, Mary."

"You're fat."

"Rosie feeds me well."

"Rosie? Who's Rosie? And where'd you meet her? No, let me guess."

"Los Angeles. She was next after you, next and last. We're married."

"Why should marriage rule her out? If you ask me, that makes her the prime suspect."

"And why lure me into a trap when I already live in one? Besides, she loves me in her way. " I pictured Rosie plopping on top of me. "We have our ups and downs."

"Relationships take work, right? Give me a break. Are you sitting around crying again 'cause you're too bored to stay and too scared to leave? Oh, well, cross her off the list, then. Who else could it be? What about the one before me, Anal?"

"Azal. A-Z-A-L."

"That's right. Iranian. Persian, I mean, like you always said. Los Angeles, too. The first was a woman in some shithole by San Francisco. Mercy's the name of the town. That, I remember. The names of women, I forget, but not the cities. I remember Bakersfield and Fresno. Then you've got the other ones, before the factory. Is that pretty much your love bio? So you're what, going backwards in time? Saving the first girl for last?"

"Pretty much."

"Why rule out your first couple of girls from Michigan? They could have moved to San Diego."

44

"That was kid's stuff. They're married now. I don't count them and I doubt they count me. Far as I can tell, everybody else is single, still under their last names, on the Internet, at least."

"So let's narrow it down. I think after me, you went back to L.A. and tried to work it out with Anal. That didn't happen, so you met this Rosie. That was that. You tired and succumbed. It's simple. Happens to everybody. But the way you used to talk about Anal tells me she's the one who sent the letter. You said she was crazy."

"Yeah, but she aced me, remember?"

"But then she probably heard you got married. An aphrodisiac for some."

"Maybe."

"So what's next?"

"Keep working backwards."

"You'll know soon as you find Anal. Or is this just an excuse to sleep around with old girlfriends?"

"Nope. But if I find Azal, I'll send her your regards."

I figured it was time to leave, but she touched my arm.

"Don't go yet. You should think about this for a while. Besides, I've got errands to run. Would you mind guarding the place while I'm gone?"

"'Guarding'?"

"Minding the store, I mean."

It was a chance to look around the apartment. I wasn't so sure I believed her yet. She seemed too interested. On the other hand, why let me stay if she had something to hide?

She stood and yawned. "I'm taking a shower. Don't worry, I won't be gone long." She made a point of closing the door behind her. But then the door opened a sliver as wide as my hope. "You're really tracking down old girlfriends on the Internet?"

"What would you do?"

Finale

"Tell myself somebody sent that letter by mistake."

The door closed. Soon, she was under the spray. Unlike me, the water still knew her body. Water found its way to places I had forgotten. Did she have a boyfriend? I was sure she would have mentioned it by now, if only to get rid of me. And did I want to sleep with her? There was no getting rid of the instinct to find out whether I could.

But sitting across from me in the director's chair was Rosie, arms crossed, smoke billowing from her nose. The chair could barely support her. She hummed a spiritual. The humming intensified. I saw a chariot with spiked wheels.

I was a married man. For all its violence and racial conflict, that marriage meant something. Like me, Rosie had a strange intelligence, one which brought no worldly rewards, only unlucky charms. Neither of us would ever be an engineer, doctor or anything else that served a purpose. Our intelligence was useless by the world's standards, but it helped us reinvent ourselves.

Sometimes we laughed at the thought we might kill one another. Our relationship absorbed that fact just as stepmothers absorb the existence of hyperactive stepchildren. But even after this short time away from Rosie, that mechanism had begun to fail. There was plenty wrong with our marriage. The grass is always greener on the other side because somebody else has to cut it. I was tired of mowing. But no matter how overgrown the grass at home, I bet any visitors would have something better to do than start the Lawnboy. Meanwhile, Mary seemed to have everything in order, each blade precisely cut. I felt wrong about it, but that didn't stop me from wanting to slip off my shoes and walk barefoot through her yard.

The door opened and Mary hurried through the crack. The towel slipped. One glimpse of that seashell ass sent Rosie crashing to the floor, the chair collapsing in my imagination, making room for pornographic visions.

Mary dressed out of sight at the end of the hallway. Then she opened the door to the little room in back. She came out with a big cardboard box that was obviously not heavy but still clumsy to carry. She set it on the floor, closed and locked the door. Who locked a bedroom door from the outside? There would be no peeking, either, as the box had been wrapped with electric tape.

She blowdried her hair and put on her makeup. When she emerged from the bathroom, it no longer seemed true I had slept with her. She was somebody else.

"I have to deliver some things. If anybody comes—I don't know, bill collector or something—just say I'm not home. Let me hear you say it."

"Mary's not home."

"Say you're my brother John."

"Okay, I'm your brother Jonathan."

"Just say John. It sounds tougher than you really are."

"Am I supposed to scare somebody off?"

"Don't be silly. I have debts. Sometimes the creditors come knocking. Starting up a business isn't cheap."

"And what business is that?"

Question ignored. She bent and felt the side of the box, as if making sure the temperature was right. Drugs came to mind, except what difference would temperature make? Then again, maybe her animal friends had been stuffed with baggies and now lived in a box.

"What happened to your stuffed toys?"

"I've got to go. I'm late already. There's food and beer in the fridge. There's whiskey in the cabinet. I don't have a TV, but you can play the stereo. And don't try looking through my computer because it's password protected."

She started toward the door and shook her head when I motioned to help. She held the box against the wall as she turned the knob.

"Why let me stay? You didn't seem so happy to see me."

"I miss TV, and you're a TV show. Route 66, maybe."

47

Finale

She slipped away. I felt bad even thinking about it, but I picked up the phone and called Rosie. I had a feeling Mary was warming to me, that I was in a choose-your-own adventure and little Johnny would get himself in deep no matter which chain of events he followed.

"Don't talk, Rosie. Let me talk for once. Let me get a word in edgewise before you start."

"So talk. I got one ear on the phone and the other next to paradise."

"What's that supposed to mean? You got somebody there already?"

"You figure it out. Caller ID says San Diego, and you're the one making accusations."

Goddamn caller ID. It was impossible to be anonymous. How did anyone get away with anything?

"You know why I'm here, Rosie, and it's not to sleep with anybody else."

"You lie easy as a whore. Your mama's been calling. Says she's worried."

"She can worry all she likes."

"You need a psychiatrist."

"I already know how I feel."

"Really? I don't think so. You're looking for clues. That's what you're doing, ain't it? Solve anything yet? Like what John plus Mary equals? You fit the rectangle in the circle yet, or did you call because you miss me?"

"Yes, that's exactly why I called."

"Well, I don't care to be missed. I'm a Mrs. and there's no reason you should be missing me other than you're missing a piece of your mind chasing white-ass windmills 'cross the countryside. She keeping you cool, providing air conditioning? Lord, I'm late for breakfast. The goddamn grill's burning."

I hung up second and was about to couch myself when someone knocked. I opened the door and saw a toolbelt.

"How's the life of leisure? I remember you now."

"Nobody called maintenance, Dennis. Need something?"

"We're supposed to keep an eye on the tenants. Management likes to get a jump on trouble. Maintenance men see a lot. We're insiders. You knock a woman around, we see the holes in the walls. You puff weed, we smell the smoke. You got something to hide, you probably stuff it in the air conditioner. Anyway, I like Mary. Tips me at Christmas."

"I like Mary, too."

"Seemed in a better frame of mind before you arrived. I saw the look on her face and figured you had something to do with it. For one thing, what's with the box? You can't lift a box for a woman? Let me guess: You've got a bad back. Boo-hoo. Mind if I take a look around?"

"You got a warrant?"

"Warrant? I can come in this apartment any time I like." He rattled the keys on his belt. "I've got about two hundred warrants right here."

He gave me a look: Watch yourself. I tried to give one back. He laughed and closed the door.

I looked around the apartment. I checked the bedroom door. It was flimsy as balsa wood, like everything else in the complex. The bathroom was a mess. She must have been doing plenty of coming and going and without much warning. Cover-all and nail polish speckled the sink, the mirror streaked with hair spray. A blowdryer lay on the floor. The shower curtain had three broken rings and sagged to the bathtub. There was another book about turtles next to the toilet.

Someone knocked. Dennis was getting on my nerves. I opened the door ready to get punched. But it wasn't him standing there.

"Thanks, I'll come inside," the Mexican said. "Who are you, Mary's boyfriend?"

"Not really."

He closed the door and said, "I'm Jesus." He had heroin skin, pockmarked, carved and stretched like an old leather belt. One thing I'd learned in the factory was that time and heroin could turn anybody American Indian, the aboriginal face of no-expenses-paid peace.

"Well, Jesus, how can I help?"

"Use the 'H', please. It's not funny. I've heard that joke a hundred thousand times."

"My wife's pretty religious, that's all. I tend to see Jesus everywhere even though I'm not much of a believer myself."

"That right? Is Mary your wife?"

Jesus touched the computer. He bent toward the manila files and rifled through them. He picked up a few, ran his finger along the columns of numbers, then dropped them, papers fluttering to the floor. He went to the kitchen and opened the refrigerator. He pushed items aside, knocking over cartons of orange juice and milk.

"Eggs," he said.

"I'm not too hungry."

He walked up to me and did not say, "Smoke 'em peace pipe?" He tugged my shirt and let go. Normally, as mentioned, I'm known as a chicken, but every once in a while I'm seized by a strange disregard for my physical health. It comes over me like another personality. Temporarily, I'm a real man. It never lasts long enough to get me into a fight, and now that I could smell his aggression, I began my usual retreat.

He said, "Where...are...eggs?"

"Listen, I don't know what you're talking about. I just got here last night. Mary's an old girlfriend. What she's doing, I have no idea. If you can find some eggs, cook 'em."

"Mary's my accountant. And she provides storage. She is not to sell on her own." He sat on the couch and rubbed his chin. "This is troubling."

"Well, let's be reasonable. She'll come back soon."

"Friend," he said with a father's disappointment, "you seem as though you could be helpful. I wouldn't want you for a friend, though."

"I'm not too brave. You're bigger than me."

"What about honor?"

"I've got no honor and I try not to judge."

"Self-respect?"

"You should hear my wife's version: 'R-E-S-P-E-C-T, best not fuck with me.' She wears the pants. Size 42."

"Jesus Christ. Friend, I'm thinking about kicking in that door back there. Are you going to jump on my back when I do it?"

"No, I'll sit right here. But I wouldn't bother kicking it; your foot might land in the next-door neighbor's living room."

He went to the door and turned it. He squatted and looked at the knob. "This is one of those locks with the bendy keys." He took a chain of keys from his pocket and inserted one. The lock gave less fight than me. "An embarrassing business, I'm in."

"And what business is that?"

"Stinks in here," he said. "But there's nothing there."

"Mind if I look?"

"I'd rather you not."

"Okay, Chief."

"I'm no Indian."

He approached, looming over me with an indecipherable expression, although I could decode enough to see it was not one of pleasure.

"I 'd be better off selling crack."

"What *do* you sell?"

"Imported food products."

"Well, it's a global economy, they say."

"I suppose so. I like that. I'll take that with me."

Finale

"You're coming back?"

"Oh, yes."

"I'll let Mary know."

"Will you be here? Perhaps we could work out a deal. Mary could use a partner. She's obviously making unwise business decisions."

"I'd think about it, but I'm not staying in the area. Some call me The Wanderer, Jesus."

"You got any money?"

"I'm not a connoisseur of imported foods. I live on pancakes, that kind of thing."

"That's not what I mean. I mean for your girlfriend. She's behind on payments. It's easy to see that she's selling behind my back and playing the unwinnable game of catch-up. Just like gamblers. I'm not violent, though, in honor of my name. My mother is very devout. But I don't consider fire, vandalism and blackmail true violence. Understand?"

"I understand. How much does she owe?"

"One thousand dollars, roughly."

I pulled out my wallet.

"Here," I said. "Let's just say Mary's out of the business."

"Yes, I think it's time I said goodbye to Mary. I'll return her stuffed animals tonight."

"Pardon me if I say that you don't seem the kind of man who keeps stuffed animals around."

"Ransom. Those goddamn things might as well be her children. Fucking Americans. So I kidnaped 'em. That's what I did because I'm a Christian criminal. Actually, 'criminal' is too impressive for what I do. I'm a waterboy in a desert, that's all." He counted the money. "Thanks to you, the animals live. I've done bad things but nothing felonious."

"Will you bring back the animals tonight?"

"I just remembered I have to make a drop at the border. Tomorrow, maybe. Will you be here?"

"I'll be gone. Why don't you leave them with the maintenance man. Tell him I left them as a gift for Mary. Make sure you dump them on the floor and take the box with you."

"I never liked that asshole, either."

"Scatter them, Jesus."

"I will scatter. Thanks for the money."

He left while I stared at the bedroom door. Now something stopped me from looking inside, but I wasn't sure I wanted to know, and then again I did.

Meanwhile, I was thinking about all the booze Mary had mentioned. Last time I'd drank, bad things happened. I shook until I thought I might split in two or start an earthquake. Before that, other bad things happened. Rosie tried to whack me, but I caught her wrist. I held it for several seconds, considering whether I might twist her arm back in retribution for all the blows I'd absorbed. But I never found out what I would have done because her free arm swung toward me, fist landing in my stomach so hard I dropped into the coffee table, smashing the glass but somehow only scraping myself on the way through.

That was our last two-way domestic incident. Rosie made me drive all the way to Gooseberry for anger management classes. There were twenty other men at the meetings, and none of them looked like they'd taken three thousand smacks in the face. I doubt they told questioning strangers their marks had been caused by falls down basement stairs, either. Rosie and I didn't even have a basement.

After that, I never drank again. Instead, I uses my imagination to fill the gaps. I became hyper-aware of sunlight and its various effects. For a long time, the world was a cubist's delight, but that effect had washed way, and it was hard to remember more had been gained than lost by quitting alcohol.

53

Finale

I went to the kitchen and opened the cabinet. I remembered the wood-barrel smell of whiskey before opening the bottle. Taking a sip would add a "Collect a Kick in the Ass" space to the Monopoly board, but the Wanderer liked his drink; he moved 'round the board in the silver automobile. Drink eased his conscience, glued his travels together into a Grandma Moses' jigsaw puzzle. I was a pastoral drunk, innocent as a valley. But the next day, life was painted by Dali.

Just then, the apartment door opened. I closed the cabinet. I heard keys drop on the floor and then I heard crying. I turned the corner to see Mary shaking and kicking like a frightened girl on a swing. I sat beside her and put my arm around her shoulder, pulling her close. I could have kissed her then, pecked her cheek in sympathy, then kissed her temple a little longer, until I finally kissed those lips already puckered in sorrow over something that must have involved our visitor from the south.

"Jesus was just here."

"Oh, John, what did he say?"

"He said 'thank you' when I gave him a thousand dollars."

"Gave him *what*?"

"I paid him off. So whatever's behind that bedroom door won't have to be there any longer. It's done. Go get a real secretary's job. Jesus is pulling a Lazarus on your stuffed animals tomorrow. Dennis will drop them off, soon as he's done picking them up off the floor. I won't even ask what it's all about. I've got my own mystery."

"A real Hardy Boy."

"I'm tired. I've had enough for one day."

"Turtle eggs."

"Huh?"

"I'll solve it for you. I deliver Mexican turtle eggs. Thieves in Mexico steal them off the coast. There's immigrants can't live without 'em, so the

54

gang smuggles the eggs across the border. I'm sure they smuggle more than that. I keep the eggs in the back room and make deliveries. If you find a little shack in the middle of nowhere, ask for turtle eggs. The waitress might laugh or she might give you a little smile and come back with endangered species on a plate. I was making one last delivery and keeping the money for myself, so I could pay them off. I don't know what I was thinking; like they wouldn't know they never got paid for that batch. Now I can't look my animals in the eyes again."

"They're stuffed."

"They know."

Now she was crying again, back to the Mary I used to know, begging to be kissed.

She said, "Jesus wasn't such a bad guy. I don't know what else he does, but to me, anyway, he's kind enough. Not that I slept with him, but he wanted to. That's how this all got started. They've got an office outside of town. I took an interview there. First, I just wrote down phone messages. Weird messages, long distance, in Spanish. Next, they asked if I could handle books. Then they asked if I could work from home. And finally they asked if I would keep something for them and make deliveries when necessary. They told me what it was; I said no. Jesus smiled and said they didn't offer unemployment benefits. He cracked his knuckles and said they didn't have Workers' Comp, either. He suggested a dumb white girl in the middle of nowhere would look innocent enough carrying a box into a restaurant and would get paid well to do it."

"But you're not dumb. Why'd you stick around in the first place?"

She snapped out of my arms, sweet Mary snuffed out, a smoldering cigarette butt in her place. "I was trying to find myself." Her shoulders slumped. She touched my face, but I jerked away. "What's the matter? Look, I'm sorry. I'm so angry at myself. Will you stay tonight, in case he comes back?"

"He won't come back, not inside this apartment, anyway. He keeps his word."

"But you need some rest for the road." She clasped my hands. "You know we've started something. Between us, I mean."

I knew she was playing me, but for what I didn't know. Still, my old violin had been in the case for a long time. It wanted new music, a little Mozart or maybe some Bach, a break in the Wagner. I had an idea, something I would do for her. Then I'd see which Mary was stronger before I decided whether to stay the night.

"I'm going for a little while," I said.

"Can't I go with you? What if he—"

"He won't come back now, but I will, in one hour. Just sit tight."

I had remembered a shopping strip around the corner, and I was hoping the store I needed was still there. It was, and they had what I wanted....what Mary needed.

I drove home with a box of my own, smaller than hers. I parked and walked up the sidewalk. The Menace was on the way out and shook his head, muttering, "Fucker." Dennis, I thought, you'll never wander far. You'll still be right here swinging your keys for the next twenty years, poking around underwear drawers but not women. I bet he knew what size Mary wore, and I had a feeling his fantasy ended with the chalk-lined form of my body.

"Don't worry, Dennis, I won't be staying long."

"Good riddance."

I imagined music boxes lined the sidewalk. For once, the String Concerto of Jonathan Thomas would not be obscured by obscene spirituals.

Mary buzzed me in and I went to her door, this time left unlocked.

"A present?"

"It's for you, to make amends." I set the box on the floor and opened the cage inside it. The turtle poked his head out, probably wondering just what the hell humans were trying to pull on him.

"What's this?"

"He'll help you forget. It's the kind of thing Jesus would do, the one with a 'J'. Not that I'm a believer."

She set it on the floor. "Run, turtle."

I swear a woman's hair can fool a man either way. Some wear a hardhat shell just like a turtle, but they're soft underneath. Others wear it long and smooth, but they're cut and tough below. Some have multiple personalities for wigs and you'd never guess they're bald. Mary was the turtle type, hidden by a flap chop or secretary's doo, trying to amputate her vulnerability but collapsing back into it at the end of the night, teddy bear at her side. Now the stuffed animals were gone and she looked at me as if I had button eyes and a furry gut. I told myself, "Watch out, John Thomas." I wasn't talking to myself, exactly, only the part that wanted one thing the rest of me did not.

She retreated toward the bed. The turtle moved along the carpet, probably wondering how long its furlough would last. He had everything but striped jail fatigues and with a few more feet of height would have wanted to shoot hoops in the sunlight. Instead, he watched me make for the bed. He looked as though he knew it was a bad idea.

"Come on," she said, patting the mattress.

"Let's not step on him. I'll put him in the cage."

"Just let him wander for a while. You of all people should know that's what he wants."

I thought of Rosie and said to myself and her, "I'm sorry, Rosie, but the way you treat me, I just can't say no to someone who speaks softly and carries no stick. I don't expect she'll slap me, nor tie me to the bedpost and leave me stranded when she's through."

Next, as always, I nearly became Mary. Sex for me is a river, taking me into the other until I become genderless. That's how I knew what to do: I did what I thought I'd want done to me if I were her. My own pleasure took care of itself. And without Rosie as a partner, sex was moonwalking, weightless. Soon, I couldn't help but wonder if I hadn't sent that letter to myself, just to land here on the lunar surface.

Mary had developed a habit of biting. She yelped and repeated my name, only now it was "Johnny, Johnny, Johnny." I hoped Dennis was eavesdropping outside the window.

I rolled away. She clamped onto my back. I could have sworn I saw Rosie's wide eyes between the bedposts.

"What's the matter?" she said. "Now you're sorry, I suppose?"

"Not sorry, just confused."

I looked over and saw the turtle in his shell; too much commotion for one day, I supposed, and I knew how he felt. It was only dusk, and I had to find a way out of that apartment.

"I could put my record on."

She ran to the boombox. We listened to artificial seashore. She sat on the side of the bed, not bothering to cover her body. I wrapped myself in blankets. One leg hung limp off the side of the bed. A figleaf in the rain, no fiddler on the roof and the violinist gone. A tree frog had leapt from her branches. It was quiet and not far away the sounds of the seashore real.

The turtle came out of his shell and wandered toward the speaker. People parked, arriving home from work. Rattling fast food bags disturbed our fraudulent surf.

Mary held herself. I must have reminded her of Flapper Mary, and she could no longer be Secretary Mary instead. She was between selves, trying to figure out which way to head. She watched the turtle move. She wouldn't look at me. I touched her back, but she shook my hand away.

"Now what, John?"

"Now?"

"Now that you're here."

I often believed people could read my mind. All this time, I thought she knew I wasn't planning to stay more than a few hours, even if this happened. I thought she knew I had a mystery to solve and my own murder to prevent. I was sure she must have guessed all of this remained foremost in my mind even while she lay naked beside me.

"Could I use your computer?" I said. "My laptop's in the car."

"Jesus Christ. Go ahead. The password's IAMMARY."

I turned on the machine and waited. She whimpered, but I had that cold feeling, one that wouldn't let me comfort her or even lie to keep things from getting worse.

The sun lit her thighs. What tricks biology played on me. I had to hang upside down to cry but also to smile. I was a bat, cold and black in my cave. I wanted to feel sorry but couldn't.

"You never know what to say, do you?"

I shook my head.

"You watch enough movies. Seems like you would know a line or two."

I started the browser and accessed my email account, screenname WANDERER6424. There was a whole world of drifters, just like, just as there were a hundred thousand men attracted to carved ducks or women with three nipples or ex-flapper girls who bit like puppies and slept on make-believe coasts. But I was number 6424, and I didn't have a thing to say in my defense.

Sure enough, there was a message from a free Internet account, email ID of IHATEJOHN. It had been sent while I was on top of Mary.

"I guess it wasn't you that sent the letter."

"No shit."

"'YOU ARE A DEAD MAN.'"

"Clever."

"It wasn't you, then?"

"Get out."

"I've got to be sure, Mary. Somebody's trying to kill me."

"Good."

I checked the details of where the message had gone to arrive at her computer, the hoops and switcharounds and turnpikes, but none of that told me anything. I searched the IP address to no effect. I printed out the letter and stuffed it in my pocket. I sat beside Mary. She inched away and started sobbing.

"I don't want you to go away."

"I know you don't, but it's only because I have to leave that you even want me to stay. A few hours ago, you practically slammed the window in my face."

She looked at me. "I do want you to stay."

"I can't."

"All right," she said, pointing at the box. "Then get the fuck out, and take that fucking turtle with you."

"Come on, Mary, he'll make you feel better."

"Did you ever see a stuffed turtle in here? I fucking hate turtles. And how do you know it's a boy?"

She pulled the sheet around her body: Show over, curtains closed. I found the turtle, put him in his cage and closed the box. I started toward the door but looked back one more time. I knew it was a boy because—because I knew, that's all.

"I bet you're really tired," she said. "I hope you fall asleep on the road and drive into a ditch."

The turtle and I left. The last thing we heard from her apartment was the recorded sounds of the sea. There was one thing left to do in San Diego, and then it was time to visit Azal.

I set the box next to me and started the car. My green friend must have been getting pretty tired of the pranks, but I had a place in mind for him. So together we drove back through the suburbs and down a stretch of road I knew. I noticed a car behind me, but there were two others and I wasn't getting paranoid yet.

When we turned down the avenue toward the beach, the car was still behind me. I spun off into a parking lot, but the other car stayed behind mine. I watched it turn around the block and figured it was a cop or maybe kids cruising for girls coming off the beach.

I took Yertle out of the car and headed for a lifeguard stand. I opened the box. I angled Yertle toward the sand. He crawled out, stopped.

"Run," I said. "Wander on."

He wasn't going anywhere. I almost wanted to take him with me, but I couldn't leave him in a box forever, and I was pretty sure the seatbelt wouldn't fit. So I stood there looking down at him, saying, "Scoot. Move. Beat it."

Headlights brightened the beach. I turned. For a second, I was blinded, but then I heard keys and tools jingling toward me. Dennis the Menace. He was carrying my suitcase, which he must have taken from my car.

"Ola," he said.

"Leave us alone."

"'Can't,'" he said, mimicking me with a soprano voice. "'I just can't.'"

"Pervert. Creep."

His sandals splattered sand. "Only the ones I love."

"But as you can see, you're not her type."

"Forget that. Here's your fucking clothes."

He flung my suitcase twenty yards into the ocean. I watched it bob away.

We stood two feet apart. I wasn't running this time. For one thing, I didn't want to step on Yertle, and for another, what little pride I had could be called to attention on rare occasions. "You forgot the laptop," I thought about saying. Instead:

"I guess you plan to hit me?"

"I was thinking about it. Guy wandering around, living off women, showing up years later like everybody owes him something. Get a job."

"I had one. I worked with ten thousand assholes just like you and then the company up and moved the factory clear down to Mexico. But I got mine before they left, so here I am. I win."

"You owe me."

"For what?"

"Mary."

Since a punch was coming, and I was running out of lines, I rushed him. I grabbed his waist and swung a quick uppercut into his waist. Instead, my knuckles caught a wrench. The skin split, but I held on while he spun me in circles, punching me in the sides until I fell off like a kid on a merry-go-round. I found my footing in the sand and retreated, trying to regain my balance. He gripped a hammer. Now murder was a real and immediate possibility. It crossed my mind Mary had sent that letter, posting Dennis outside the door to carry out my sentencing when I left, just as she had predicted would occur.

But he let go of the hammer. He came at me and hit me in the face. The headlights spraypainted the black sky in my head, my brain a satellite flown amok. I crash landed on the beach. The true sounds of the ocean made a fine static...until the world began to move.

Earthquake 2.0

Birth: wallop; light; surplus skin...Land ho.

Clouds, wind, drizzle: "Director-style," she said.

She of whiskey mountain, high after dusk,

loosely of the Biblical persuasion.

I rise, wide-eyed at the worldwide conflict.

I fear but hear animal messages.

No felonies, minus imagining.

I remain question stuffed, query weighted.

Who invented the lightbulb, aeroplanes?

We build fate with help from the mystical.

We come from cracked eggs, turtle time, no shell.

"Accept it," they say, except I'm breakfast.

I go soprano, singing in my sleep.

On the way out: frogs; sun; Indians; blood.

No, don't speak of fate; don't speak of choices.

Six

Later, I always remembered those reveries. I tried to read between the lines. I parsed the words. I added them up and divided by the lowest common denominator. I never worked out the answer; the problem was wrong. If I was a student, my professor was wicked, chalking unsolvable equations on the blackboard of my mind, and the trail always ran cold.

So did mornings on a San Diego beach. People from Michigan confuse Southern California with Tahiti. They think the morning begins with coffee served in cocoanut shells. True, California can be easy in the right circumstances, but when life capsizes, blue skies become a saddening device, rubbing it in like love songs at the grocery store when you've just been dumped. If things go wrong in the west, you hope for rain or snow to match the mood, for everybody else to bitch about the weather and turn surly in the slush. In Michigan, misery never lacks company.

But there was no surcease when I awoke with sand in my nose and saw jet exhaust above. The first thing I did was search for Yertle, but I must have disgraced him: He was gone. Instead, a surfer made his way toward me. He parked his board above my head, bare toes three inches from my face.

"You look like a lawyer. You don't wanna sleep down here at night. Should I call an ambulance?"

Jaw still out of service, I shook my head and waved him off.

A minute later, he rode a wave. I sat up and watched. He was a porpoise; I was a frog. He caught another wave straight toward the coast. He glared at me, probably thinking, "What'd I just tell you? Get lost." The wave delivered him to shore. He scrambled through the water and back toward me.

"What's the problem?"

"Some jerk KO'd me last night. I blacked out right here. What is this, private property?"

"Semi-private. It's our turf this time of day. I had a little wake-up smoke this morning. Fact is, you're distracting me."

I tried to stand but lost my balance. He held out a hand and lifted me.

"Come on, find your legs."

"I'd rather find a shower."

He pointed toward to a building a mile in the distance.

"That's a public beach house. They've got showers."

I patted my pockets. "It's not gonna cost me fifty cents or something, is it? All the change fell out of my pockets."

"Shit, man, are you indignant or something?"

"Yes, I'm pretty indignant right about now."

"Then you're better off in Los Angeles. You see how clean this beach is?"

"All right, I'm leaving. I don't suppose I can drive down there?"

"This is the closest parking lot. You'll have to walk."

"Would you do me a favor? If you see a suitcase out there in the sea, it's mine."

My feet sunk in the sand. The drag made me feel like Lawrence of Arabia on his way through the desert. When I looked back, the surfer was calling someone on a cell phone, probably a semi-private beach patrol to make sure I left after the shower.

I counted my steps, trying to take my mind off the body's complaints. "You're going to that shower," I told myself. "March."

Then I saw Yertle. He looked at me and shook his head. Okay, he didn't, but he might as well have, for he just sat there with a look of contempt.

Finale

"Come on, Yertle. Follow me."

He wasn't going anywhere.

"Be that way, then."

Finally, I made it to the building. By some miracle, the door was unlocked. I brought my clothes with me into the stall. The water stung. I cringed in the downpour. I squeezed what lather I could from the sliver of soap and made sure the suds fell on the clothes at my feet.

After about ten minutes, I held my garb in the spray, then turned off the water and squeezed the bundle as dry as I could. I left the stall and took the clothes to the air-blower. I stood naked for another fifteen minutes and said a Rosie-like prayer that no one come inside.

I waited until everything stopped dripping. I dressed and looked in the mirror. The clothes were still damp and even more wrinkled, but my vision was a little clearer now, mind out of neutral. I began to feel I could turn away from the night before, toward today...even if my reflection looked like a mugshot.

Outside, it was warmer. What I wanted to do was lay in the sun and let the clothes finish drying while I caught another hour or two of sleep. But when I looked down the beach, I saw that four more surfers had gathered in a circle, a mini-conference about indigence on the beach. They stared in my direction. I looked behind and saw a steep hill between myself and the road, but it was the only surfer-free path back to my car.

Somehow, I made the distance. Then I noticed the scratches on my car, spelling "ASSHOLE" across the entire width of the hood. I imagined Dennis with a fistful of keys, grooving his message so deep it sparkled. I considered camouflaging the word with more scratches, but I didn't have the strength.

I fell into the car and drove as far as I could down the coast, toward the next lot. I parked with the rear of the car facing the sun and climbed into the back seat. Dennis was probably wrapping his toolbelt around his waist right now. Mary was probably reading the advice column in the newspaper:

Dear Fran:

Last night my old boyfriend visited me. You can guess what
happened and now I feel like a whore. I don't know how to
forget about him and move on with my life, and I'm worried
he might come back. What should I do?

Signed,

"Tiffany" in San Diego

Ola, "Tiffany" in San Diego:

Don't beat yourself up over bad choices. With any luck,
he fell asleep on the road and drove into a ditch. Or maybe
he got his ass kicked on a semi-private beach. If he comes
back, tell him to get the fuck out and take his fucking
turtle with him.

For about five minutes, I recharged while considering events. It wasn't
impossible Mary really had set everything in motion. I remembered Dennis
holding the hammer. Maybe he backed out of murder but felt comfortable
enough with aggravated assault. Maybe afterwards, when he got home, he
reconsidered homicide, returning the next morning to finish me off. He
would find my car gone, but the surfer would say, "Yeah, I know who you're
talking about. He went to that beach house down there. He was looking pretty
rough, so he couldn't have gone far. I bet he went back to his car and drove
to the next parking lot because I let him know this is semi-private property
in the a.m. hours." Now Dennis was probably parked on the other side of the
lot, waiting for me to fall asleep. Then he'd run a hose from the exhaust pipe
into the backseat, start the ignition, lock the doors, roll the windows tight. As
a last gesture, he would amend my hood tattoo: "DEAD ASSHOLE."

Finale

I was getting paranoid. I tried to relax and fade.

Yertle was in the front seat. He looked back at me and said, "Don't worry, I'll do the driving. You sleep."

But I was dreaming, so tired the earth held steady.

When I awoke, everything fell out of place. I'd spent over half my money in one stop. There had been plenty of activity, but nothing had been solved. It was back to Los Angeles now. What I wanted was a motel, but I couldn't spare the cash, not this soon, not with L.A. only a few hours away.

I would have to hope Azal let me through the door. Maybe she still had some of my clothes in a box, though they had more likely been set ablaze long before.

Azal was a vengeful woman. Acts she had committed against me—or seemed to commit—had stained my memory. And yet of all the women in my past, she had come closest to understanding the true Jonathan Thomas. She knew why weak men love Raymond Chandler. What I considered weak, she called "a unique femininity." She wanted me to let it shine, sister. Then, just when I thought I knew what she wanted, she expected gravitas. When it came to gravitas, I was weightless. Not even lead boots could make me stand a confrontation.

In the end, she had me masochistic enough to endure Mary and mean enough to leave her the way I had. There must be spells woven into Farsi for all the Persian torment I endured from Azal. I learned the meaning of cuckold and went cuckoo. Now I was going back. Dennis must have hit me in the head with that hammer.

I stopped at a restaurant and asked for hard-boiled eggs. The waitress looked at me as if I'd demanded turtle eggs. I should have ordered them scrambled in honor of my brains.

Afterward, I bought cigarettes. It was no coincidence I picked a liquor store. I stared at the array of intoxicants. There was rum for the sun, gin for the moon, wine for quiet, whiskey for noise, vodka for hangovers. For breaks, there was beer. I drank a lot during the factory years and sometimes after. When I had problems living, intoxication made a fine substitution.

"Something else?" the clerk said.

"Just thinking."

"It's not a library."

I felt myself on the shore of alcoholic memory, toes touching the sand.

"No, nothing else."

It was a some experience driving down the highway with "ASSHOLE" glowing on the hood of my car. A family of three returning home from Disneyland lost count at two-thousand bottles of beer when they saw and pointed, mother shielding the child's eyes. I kept wondering if a cop would pull me over. There must have been a law against epithets on cars, Statute 35446.2.2.1.1.2.4(A): "Driving a vehicle with the word 'ASSHOLE' painted, drawn, scratched or in any other manner displayed on its exterior shall be a misdemeanor punishable by 30 days in jail, a fine of up to [one dollar more than whatever I had in my wallet], or both."

I'd tell the judge I was in trouble, that'd I'd received two threatening letters in as many days and had no one to protect me. "Besides, Your Honor, who would scratch 'ASSHOLE' on the hood of his own car?"

Somehow, I squinted through the headache and smoked enough cigarettes to keep my eyes open. Every now and then, the car drifted across the lanes, but once again I would disappoint Mary; I wasn't driving into a ditch just yet. The trip seemed to last a hundred years, the task of keeping the car straight as challenging as it had been when I used to drive drunk.

Soon, I was on the outskirts of Los Angeles. I remembered the way to Azal's house in Sherman Oaks. I'd been thrown out of that house so often it was best to focus on this humiliating return there. I had taken this street, and then that street, and then this street, the air conditioning broken. The sun would bear down on me. I would shield my face, for fear a sign on my forehead indicated, "Property of Azal."

I hit the gas, worried I might collapse any minute. Down her street. Christ. I swerved into the driveway, tires screeching, careening into memory, the future and the back of her Mercedes.

The crunch of bumpers did little to her car, but mine smoked. My head hit the steering wheel, producing bruise on bruise. I climbed out of the car and for a second the world became a Persian carpet, designs echoing within each other, the reverberations creating new designs.

I braced myself against the car. My feet gave way and the back of my head clanked a hubcap. I dropped through a metallic mandala, decentered, lost in a fractal.

"Azizam, nakon," she said, rubbing my head.

Azal helped me inside as best she could; she was little, brain bigger than her body. I was conscious when I passed through the frame of the door I knew so well. Then I lay on the couch. She draped blankets across me. I felt like a vanquished king. She sat next to me. I thought I heard her say, "They warned me," but I didn't know what that meant. Was she the assassin?

She pulled the blanket over my eyes. I regenerated in the cocoon even as I wondered if it might be a coffin made of cloth.

"Sleep, my baby boy."

My jaw still hurt too much to smile. But underneath that blanket, I would have died content. This was the way to die, not knowing anything, nor believing anything with certainty, like a humbled physicist.

"Shut up and sleep," I said to myself.

"Azizam, nakon."

The mandala ceased its spreading and folded back into me. For just a moment, I felt whole. It might have been the beating I'd taken. I realized all my questions only led to more questions. The streaks of color in my eyes evaporated into blackness. For a second, I saw the word "ASSHOLE" and then I imagined Azal faithfully buffing it out of the hood. Then I heard myself snoring.

When I awoke, Azal had breakfast spread on the coffee table, deserts and breads, lemonade and orange juice, a cloth napkin. I couldn't help but look around at this house that had left me behind, or the other way around, as I could still hear the water trickling from the indoor waterfall, into which a kind of canal poured, having traveled all the way around the room to get there. I remembered the first time I'd seen it:

"There's a freaking aqueduct in your living room."

The Shah of Iran still stared down at me, as he had years before. These were not the Iranians who had taken Americans hostage in the 1970s; these were the ones who would have helped hostages escape in exchange for tickets to America. Still, the Shah, even if dead, didn't fuck around, and he looked none too thrilled at my return.

I said, "You live alone now?"

"Mommy and daddy died back in—"

A year apart from each other. Yes, I knew. I don't know why I asked. I'd looked them up on the Social Security database. Every now and then I thought of Azal, knew that her father had a weak heart, her mother's weaker. I always suspected that when her parents died, Azal would go insane—more insane. But she looked fine.

"I've accepted it," she said. "Eat. Do I look older?"

"No," I lied. She looked as if her parents had wrinkled into her. "I'm sure I do."

"You've still got a little girl's complexion. With stubble. But you can shave later. First, tell me why you're here. Especially when I sent you that letter that you never answered."

Christ, it *was* Azal. Big surprise. She had threatened me before. Sometimes during arguments, she'd start shaking like an engine about to explode. One night, she called the cops after I threw the phone at the wall. "I'm going," I told the cops, waving at them—"Tootles"—as I walked out the door and down the street. For some reason, they didn't stop me. I kept walking and slept in a park that night. No one woke me up and said I looked like a lawyer. No one woke me at all because I couldn't sleep, surrounded by the indignant, some of whom boxed invisible opponents in the dark. The next morning, I searched for a water fountain, even one dripping with hepatitis, until I finally found a McDonalds and begged a cup of water.

"You sent that letter? I knew it."

"Knew it? You knew my parents died and never answered?"

"Azal, where did you send that letter to?"

"To your mother's house. I figured she'd forward it."

"My mother wouldn't forward a donated kidney."

I took the letter from my pocket and handed it to her.

"Oh," she said. "Somebody doesn't like you very much."

"Not you, though? And then there's this."

I handed her the printed email.

"Oh, my. You don't think I sent this?"

"I don't know who sent it. Obviously, it's from an ex-girlfriend. You're an ex-girlfriend. I had to check. Wouldn't *you*?"

"I would have figured it's from a crazy person."

"I guess everybody but me takes death threats in stride."

"And who's everybody? I'm not the first you visited? You saw Mary what's-her-name first?"

"Yes, Mary first. I'm going backwards in time."

"And how is she?"

"Hasn't found the Great Gatsby yet."

"It's a daisy chain."

"A what?"

"Nothing. What happened to your face?"

"I ran into somebody's fist."

"Are you tired? Do you want to sleep some more?"

"Shower. And some clothes, if you have anything."

"I think so. I'll look around while you're in the bathroom."

I took my second shower that day. This time, I didn't have to worry whether somebody was going to wander in and notice my laundry next to my feet. The spray felt good, like I was starting over again, with new skin and muscles. In the hum of water, I wasn't thinking so much about Rosie, nor was I imagining sex with anybody else. I felt genderless, a pre-born creature. That water must have come from the River Jordan, the way it restored me, and I felt good about myself for the moment. Look what I'd done for Mary. I felt so damn refreshed under the water that I started singing a G-rated version of Rosie's favorite:

"You and me, we sweat and strain,
"Body all achin' and racked with pain.
"Tote that barge and lift that bail,
"You get a little drunk and you lands in jail.
"I gets weary, and sick of trying.
"I'm tired of livin', but I'm scared of dyin'.
"But Ol' Man River, he just keeps rollin' along."

Azal knocked on the door and said, "Silly." She said things like that, phrases phased out of usage. She restored them. They took on a certain Azal-ness—ESL magic.

There was a big towel hanging over the shower door, as if she'd been expecting company. I dried off. It was still chilly and the bathroom heater

73

was cooking. I stood in front of the vent. It was better than a massage or spa or full-body transplant.

She opened the door and tossed some clothes inside. I put on a red golf shirt, khaki pants, argyle socks. I looked like a 60-year-old man, one who owned an iron. A 9 iron, to be exact.

Then I thought, "Sixty: Wasn't that when her—"

"You look good in Daddy's clothes. Now I'm glad I didn't get rid of them."

"You could have kept mine."

"Salvation Army. Leave your other clothes right there. I was going somewhere today, and I thought you might come with."

She told me where.

"You mean you want me to wear your father's clothes to his own grave?"

"What does he care? He can't wear the clothes. He'll laugh."

"You want me to go to a cemetery practically carrying a bag of golf clubs on my back? Should I yell, 'Fore!' when we get there?"

She started crying.

"What's the matter?"

"He was playing golf when it happened."

Now I remembered: This was the anniversary of the day he died. Out of three hundred and sixty-five fucking days, I picked this one. And only Azal would consider putting me in her father's golf clothes for a graveside chat.

"Come on," I said, knowing I would agree whether or not I bothered arguing first, "let's get it over with."

"Really?"

We went to my car. In the glare, my "ASSHOLE" burned.

"Nice."

"Where we headed?"

"Slauson. Holy Cross Cemetery."

"Wasn't he Muslim?"

74

"How many times do I have to explain that we're secular?"

"Isn't Catholicism a sect?"

"Just drive, okay, Johnny?"

She was the only one to often call me Johnny. Underneath her usual talk lay this other language: cartoonish; girly; lovable. I guess that was her nonsecular side, crafted in Catholic private schools, where she must have been the only Iranian with black Shirley Temple hair, more American than the Angelenos whom she insisted call her Lisa...so they wouldn't know her heritage.

While I drove, I wondered if I had an out-of-wedlock child somewhere. It wasn't impossible. I'd never worried much about preventing it, although a father was the last thing I was meant to become, if I was meant to become anything. I couldn't raise myself nor the dead and certainly not the newborn. I lacked the gene. But I supposed the government would have found me by now.

We cut through the traffic, mostly convertibles so imported they did everything but blow European cigarette smoke out their exhaust pipes. And the highways: I had gotten lost in that town so many times that I learned to steer by the relative position of the Hollywood Hills. I would even get lost on the way to Azal's apartment on Formosa, where we lived in total secrecy. Never was I allowed to answer the telephone, in case her mother called and discovered we lived together. She was every bit as seductive as Azal, with a voice that rolled out like Aladdin's carpet. I wondered if charm ran in the family or was a national trait. Such questions I once considered when trying to find my way home to an address under which only one of us was officially listed.

"We had a funny relationship," Azal said as we plunged into L.A. proper.

"Things were difficult. I was indignant, then."

"You mean indigent."

"As a matter of fact, I'm close to broke now. My wife has the money, not me. I'm not sure I have her, either."

Finale

"I knew you'd get married after me. Who is she?"

"Rosie."

"Rosie? And what is she?"

"About three-hundred pounds of trouble."

"I mean what nationality?"

"Some kind of black."

"Why do you talk that way? Can't you say African-American?"

I always wondered what it would be like to come back. For some reason, I never saw the L.A. everyone else hates. To me, it was still a Spanish outpost, even if it had been occupied by two million assholes.

We cruised into the cemetery, which thankfully was almost empty. We passed one Hispanic family, who stopped and pointed at my car. One of them took something from a purse.

We went around the curving road all the way to the back of the lot. We parked in the shade of a tree and climbed out. I had everything but a golfball and tee as we walked toward the graves. There were three of them in a row.

"That's Granny, and that's Daddy, and that's Mommy."

I was afraid she would start crying again, but instead she swept cuttings from the stones. She squinted and seemed to think not about but *at* the dead. She smiled, and I knew she felt something graves never made me feel. Since visiting them as a child, I've never understood the process. If you believe in heaven, the dead are everywhere. If you don't, they're nowhere. Either way, they're not where you're standing. It's disgusting. And it takes up room. Besides, I would rather rifle through a dead man's closet. Clothes are closer to the dead than bones.

"Are you all right?"

"I'm fine. Why shouldn't I be?"

"Cemeteries give me the creeps."

"They're supposed to give you the creeps."

"I don't want the creeps."

"They'll bury me right here next to Mommy. You won't visit?"

"That's enough."

"Mommy died in the shower, with the water running. Daddy couldn't stand being away from her, so he drowned in her."

Her father had been a magician in Iran and even performed at The Magic Castle in Hollywood. But I think he was also supposed to be a real magician, for Azal once claimed he had the cure for cancer stored in his refrigerator. Well, I learned not to ask too many questions. "Okay," I'd tell myself, "he's got the cure for cancer in his refrigerator."

I wanted to get the hell out of there, and my chance was coming straight at us in the form of a pickup truck loaded with lawn maintenance equipment.

The driver pulled alongside my car, parked, climbed out slowly. He looked at the hood of my car. He looked at me. I could hardly see him in the sun. He nodded. I nodded.

"You can't park this car here."

"I understand. Just so you know, I didn't put that word there."

Azal turned away from the dead. I knew what was coming, and it would be live.

"We can park here if we want."

"No, ma'am, you can't park a car with the word 'asshole' on the hood."

"He didn't write it."

"He just told me so."

"Then we can park here."

"No, you can't."

"It's okay, Azal. We'll just go."

"I'm not ready to go. Fuck this guy. We can fucking park here if we want."

"Lady, you can't park a car with a swear word on it in the middle of a cemetery."

"Why the fuck not?"

"Because it's a cemetery."

"I know it's a fucking cemetery. That's my mother, father and grandmother right there. They don't give a shit about a word on a car."

"Azal."

"Fuck this asshole."

"Listen," he said, "must I call the police? I'd rather not."

"Go ahead and call," Azal said. "There's no regulation about parking a car with a motherfucking swear word on it."

"I think there might be," I said.

"Then let him call. I don't give a shit."

"Fine," he said.

He got into his truck and drove back to ghost headquarters.

"Let's go," I said.

"I'm not done."

"Pray in the car."

"I'm not going."

"Yes, you are. We're going. Get in that car or I'll leave you here."

"Go ahead."

It was just like the old days, only before she always held the keys and I was the stranded one. I started the engine and rolled down the passenger-side window.

"Get in."

"No."

"Azal: Get in."

She mouthed "no." I backed up the car, but I couldn't do it. I didn't have the—I don't know what I didn't have, but I couldn't do it.

"Let's go before the cops come."

She stomped toward the car.

"Just take me home."

"Fine."

"Just like he said: 'Fine.'"

"Fine."

Dust trailed us out of the cemetery. I imagined a train of skeletons tied to the exhaust pipe, tibias and femurs bouncing off the road, skulls pitching into the air and rolling to a stop fifty feet behind us. I couldn't help but wish one of them belonged to my mother, not the real one but the Other. That was one of Azal's phrases, "the Other," acquired in undergrad, expanded upon in grad school, which I would have bet ten thousand dollars she still attended. She was studying philosophy, or—more or less accurately—phenomenology of the feminist hieroglyphic. Some bullshit. It was an elaborate stitching of her own tapestry, the threads drawn so tightly together that no light poured through, the illusion sealed. Once again, I remembered why I loved and hated her. Somewhere between Silly and the Other was an undiscovered Azal. I was telling myself even then, "Don't go digging. It's a desert. You've got no map."

"How's the studying going?"

"I'll be done in a year. I've been off since this all happened."

"I'm sure you'll catch up."

"I'll do *fine*."

She wasn't alone; there was a fury in me, too, dehydrated by heat. A litany of bars came to mind, where my old religious ceremonies had been performed a thousand times after incidents like these.

I would get drunk and call Azal from a pay phone, but we never worked out even a stalemate, much less a treaty. I'd slam the phone and drink more, then call her back. She'd get angrier. Finally, I'd go home and wait for her to arrive back from wherever she had fled. I'd pass out waiting. Who knew where she went? Maybe back to her parents, or possibly to see one of her numerous male "friends." She provided suspicious patterns, like wanting to go to parties and pretend we weren't a couple. She was a lot like drinking;

the more shit she gave me, the more I accepted, and I refused to see what she was doing to me, always telling myself next time would be better.

If she were driving, it was guarantee written in ten thousand rials that she would have skidded to a stop and demanded I get out of the car. I would have been trapped in the middle of some suburb, without a cab in sight and buses that arrived once every two hours and took another two hours to go around the block. But I was in control this time, and we were going home. Smoke all but poured from her ears, toot-toot, the train ready to slide off the tracks any second. She was scorched. We were a match and not one made in heaven.

We pulled into the driveway.

"Now what?"

"What do you mean, 'Now what?' Get the fuck out and happy travels."

"You can let me stay one night, can't you? On the couch?"

"On Daddy's couch, you mean?"

"It's your couch now, Azal. Everything gets repossessed at death. He'd want you to have it."

She got out of the car. I knew she wanted to see if I had the balls to follow her inside. And for once, I did, but it wasn't courage. The next stop was a longer drive, and I didn't have it in me yet. In two days, I had done more traveling than I had in years. At home, a trip to the john was a decathlon. Here in the haze, with enough tremble for another minor earthquake, I needed respite.

When I met her at the door, she opened it without a word. I went inside and fell on the couch. She sat in a chair across from me, shaking her head.

"The personal is the political," she said. "Everything is political."

"Oh, Christ. That guy was doing his job. Those people we passed on the way to the grave must have hopped on their cell phones like Mexican jumping beans. 'Pendejos on the loose,' they told the guy in the truck. Then the guy in the truck had to make us leave. And if we wouldn't have left, he

80

would have called the cops. Then some bull-legged asshole would have come at us with that goddamn look cops have—it's commonsense, what I did."

"No, it's political."

Every once in a while, I understood the apelike urge for violence, that desire to smack somebody over the head with a bone. I had experienced that feeling often with Azal, and I was experiencing it again. She stymied me. She stifled. She rifled my brain with a shotgun. She shot me full of holes and laughed when the light poured through. I was a duck in a permanent hunting season.

Then, out of nowhere, as if to test me again, she said, "Let's do it."

"Do what?"

She unbuttoned her shirt. Oh, no, not this time. Not Johnny, Jonathan, and especially not John Thomas.

"It's not a good idea that we get involved."

"Who wants to get involved?"

"I'm tired."

"I'll do everything."

Now I understood: This *was* political. It was about anything but sex. She climbed beside me and the fumbling began.

"Maybe I *am* the one trying to kill you," she whispered, but she probably considered this a hermeneutical exploration of the linguistic applications of sadomasochistic encounters on the Oedipal couch. I should have checked my feet for footnotes. But I was giving in, letting it happen.

Suddenly, with more force than I meant to exert, I pushed her off me. She bounced on the floor. Her head missed the coffee table, but she looked at the glass her face had almost struck, and then she looked at me.

"Abuse."

"Give me a break."

"That was no accident." She pointed at the Shah. "My uncle used to work for SAVAK. You know what SAVAK is?"

Finale

"Yeah, yeah, the Shah's secret service. They couldn't put him back together again so they came here. They're gas station attendants now, right? Or liquor store merchants? I've bought a few bottles from an ex-torturer or two. I suppose you're threatening me?"

"That's right. Now get the fuck out of here. And take off those clothes. You're not taking them with you."

I changed in the bathroom. When I came out, I saw that for some reason, she was headed for the garage. I ran to my car, but when I tried to start it, the engine wouldn't turn.

I watched the garage door open, an aluminum curtain. I saw her feet. The car still wouldn't start. I saw the rest of her. She was holding a can. The ignition still couldn't make it over the hill. Now she was coming at the car. The engine almost obeyed when I tried again but then it chortled and quit on me. I turned the key one more time as she tore off the can's lid and sent a torrent of blue at my hood, adding "F-U-C-K-I-N-G" above "A-S-S-H-O-L-E."

"What the fuck—"

The engine rumbled. I backed out of the driveway, but she came at me, grabbing the door and spaying my face. She covered my left cheek before her hand fell off the door and I sped out of there.

I could still see her in the sideview mirror. She did not appear any nearer than she actually was; she was as far as she could be.

"Azizam, nakon," I said, waving at her retreating image.

If this were a blue-sunned planet, I had a farmer's tan. I wiped away another tear. I'm a goofy bastard, driven by a conscience with weight but no power, a cracked engine block. It seemed to me that everything was justified if I added one column of figures and not the next. Azal and I had argued about our vantagepoints until they intersected into this road I once again took away from her.

I'm no mechanic. I stopped at a hardware store and bought a can of spraypaint and some thinner. Outside the store, I splashed the thinner on my face and wiped it off with my shirt. I headed to my FUCKING ASSHOLE car as the people in the lot watched.

"Sorry, Dapple," I said, for I realized this old donkey of a car was as loyal a friend as I possessed. Then I uncapped the paint and disguised the hood as best I could. My car looked like it had emerged from a chop shop. My face was red with chemical burn.

Night in the distance, I needed to stop, to wait and let it all sink into my bottomless head. There was one thing to do, and I knew where it would happen, and I knew what I would do while it happened. I just didn't know what would happen afterwards. That could not be predicted.

I drove back to Los Angeles. On the way to the Formosa Bar, I stopped in front of our old apartment. It was a pale blue building, square, with a crab grass for a lawn and a cockroach zoo for a trash dumpster. There were two floors. It was a place where everyone banged on the walls for quiet when they were done making noise. Above our old apartment, some kid used to make enough racket for Wimbledon.

One time, I awakened to an earthquake. A real earthquake. The walls leaned. I thought it was the alcohol until knick-knacks fell from the shelves. Azal wasn't home when it happened. I wouldn't doubt she conjured that earthquake. I would leave her soon after that, or at least left before she could leave me.

I always wondered how I would feel if I returned to this place. Five minutes was enough to realize.

I went around the corner to the drugstore on Santa Monica Boulevard. I picked up a crime novel, the only choice Elmore Leonard. They call him a Detroit novelist, but he hails from Birmingham, Michigan. It might have been twenty minutes from Detroit, but his town was to the Motor City as Beverly Hills is to Compton. Those cons he invented walked not the quiet streets of Birmingham. The cons in that suburb made their money the old-fashioned way, legally, on dopes like me pulling levers, until they moved their factories to Mexico. But I just wanted story, anybody's but my own. Something fast, something that might get my mind back in line with my own plot. I was losing the threads of that plot. They were coming apart faster than those of my thinner-soaked T-shirt.

When I pulled into the Formosa lot, it was like smoking that first cigarette at the start of my journey. It all came back to me. Somehow I knew I would end up at this bar again, which, within walking distance of the apartment, had served as my getaway on a hundred occasions.

I said to myself, "This is a mistake, Jonathan Thomas."

Is there anything one can do but sidle up to a bar? How many teetotalers sit at counters watching baseball or listening to Mustang Sally for the ten-thousandth time? Yes, this moment had been sneaking up on me with its usual soft-shoe routine, and I accepted its advance.

We the sidling look for cracks in time. We try to form a fault line between one day and the next. We climb down ropes like geologists digging for gems. Everything glimmers and shimmers, the walls of the fissure packed with rubies, sapphires, emeralds, tanzanite. At the bottom of the pit, somebody sings a torch song. The lights are dim. We think of our Azals and Marys and Rosies, the gemstones of our memory, which we've lost or pawned. In their place: Zirconia.

Witnessing my approach this time was not a photo of the ex-Shah but celebrities, autographed photos winking: "Welcome back, compadre." A goddamn Greek chorus of Jack Benny, Clark Gable, Liz Taylor, Jack Webb. Any second, they would emerge from their frames, lift a drink in my honor and sing a song of mourning...for tomorrow morning.

"What'll it be?" the bartender asked, because that's the way some L.A. bartenders speak, with lines from screenplays their customers write after getting drunk.

"Gin and tonic."

Bubbles, lime...as always. I cracked my book—cracked because I was still that geologist with my chisel—and began reading. Some cheap Florida scam, with wise-acre lines and a fast-moving plot, more script than novel, quick as the jets and subways on which it was read. Perfect. It took my mind off the tap on my wallet through which poured a stream of ten dollar bills.

A woman sat beside me. It could not be said she was my type. As noted, my type was broadly defined. They wore the pants, delivered slaps, swore more than I did, took a lot of shit but charged heavy interest. They came in every shade of skin, every body size, and in each case maintained metaphysical beliefs that stretched reason like a broken rubberband, the better with which to snap me in the ass. That was my type. It wasn't a type at all.

Black hair draped her shoulders in wiglike shards.

The bartender delivered a drink to her and said, "Here you go, Lemon."

"Lemon?" I said, turning my book over. "Never heard that one before."

"Lemon fresh."

"Just asking."

"You don't like it?"

"I'm a lime man."

"But you can make lemonade out of—"

Here we go, I thought. I was already drunk. Four drinks and I was cooked. It must have been chemical nostalgia, my brain sprinting through the airport to embrace its long-lost, abusive lover. They embraced and kissed but in two hours would fling lamps at each other.

For now, though, everything was yes, yes, yes, yes, yes, yes, yes. The United Nations had forged an international peace treaty, written on a bar napkin.

"You got a car?" she said.

"Mmm."

"Go for a ride?"

Finale

Lemon. Did I care she was a prostitute? Did I even want sex? I only wanted my mystery to solve itself, reach an equal sign, but it was multiplying. I was dealing in algorithms when simple math was challenge enough for this calculator.

Tomorrow, I would drive to the next suspect's location, northward and further back in time. But not now, not yet.

I said to myself, "This is a mistake, John Thomas." Then I said to her, "Let's get a motel."

"Mmm. Sunset's cheapest."

"We don't have to talk this way We don't have to talk, period."

Twenty minutes later, after stopping to pick up a fifth of gin, we lay on the motel bedspread.

"Money first."

I paid. We fiddled. We faddled. She reached inside. She said something like, "You feel a little...little. Sorry—I shouldn't have said that."

I thought every woman on earth knew better than to tell a man that. But I was too busy reaching inside her pants to comment.

"Don't think you want to do that."

Right. Because what I touched was not a plum nor a peach and certainly not a rose.

"Get out."

He looked hurt. "I thought you knew."

"I should have. You got your money. Now get out."

He found his purse and left. I checked to make sure my wallet remained in place. I peeked through the curtains to confirm he kept walking. It wasn't too far back to Santa Monica and LaBrea.

Now the manager who had registered us—a Persian, I was sure, because I can spot them from here to Iran—carried a deposit bag to his car. I yanked the curtains shut and took a drink. I had to bury one thought before passing out: "SAVAK, sent by Azal."

Paranoia is in the eye of the beholder.

Should I tell my dream, describe it in all its mustachioed glory, complete with slit throats courtesy of SAVAK, Azal hovering, a piano named Rosie dropping from a window and landing on me with the sounds of detuned strings, and a guy named Jesus smashing turtle eggs in my face? Shrapnel REM, dreams splintering like logs chopped by Paul Bunyan.

Not another alcoholic's memoir? No, I'll spare all but the requisite detail, like this: I was a fly, warned by other flies, "Niner, niner, pest strip ahead." And yet I whipsawed near the stick, knowing I was getting close from the moment I stared at those bottles in the liquor store, longing to glue my story tight with the lubrication on my hands from a slide down the tubes.

Now it was two in the morning. I drank more, putting myself down. A minor panic nipped my toes: Who was next? Shit, I could barely remember. What town was it? I had to remember I was going backwards.

First was Rosie, or should I say last? And before her Mary, and before her Azal. I'd traveled south when I first came through California those many years before. I met Azal in Los Angeles, then went down to San Diego for Mary, then come back for Azal but ended up with Rosie. But who preceded Azal? Which one was it? Which town? Which goddamn town?

Because when I first came to California, I arrived at a resort in this little town south of San Francisco called Mercy. If the mystery would not solve itself before then, that would be my last destination, home of the first girl of my travels, named Holly but also known as Holly Gonightly, with good reason. Her flag demanded, "Please tread on me." She always kept it raised. It was a trap, and two husbands fell into it. She couldn't help it; there was something spidery about her, except two of her legs were more than enough. Every man who met her, including me, thought for a moment that he might be her last, but it was always the other way around.

Then, I remembered. The next stop north was the mutant offspring of

Finale

Alabama and the Sahara, born in Southern California. Bakersfield, that is. For Christ's sake, I was going to Bakersfield. According to my information, that was still home of Kerrie, this Japanese girl—okay, woman, but more girl than woman—who loved speed and comic books, in that order. A throwback to Sun, only born in the States, acclimated if dislocated. How the hell did a cool metal thing like Kerrie end up in a smelting pot like Bakersfield? And what might she hold against me to send such a letter? She couldn't give a fuck if you punched her in the face, long as you had some meth on your knuckles.

"Christ, let me sleep."

Finally, I did fall asleep. When I awoke, the manager was knocking on my door.

Let me say this about dreams: Who gives a shit? So a metal dog bit my ankles? So it had a steel mustache? So the dog wore a toolbelt? So it had tits and a dick and humped my leg no matter how many times I kicked it off? So Jesus with a "J" was sitting on the sofa laughing his cross off and telling me to cool it and let the dog have its day? Who gives a shit because the light breaks in and all you've got to show for eight hours is a jigsaw puzzle that comes apart in radiation? You start the day exploded view and try to put yourself back together. And if you're lucky, somebody isn't knocking on the door, kick-starting a hangover.

"You leave now," he said. "Twelve-thirty. Check-out time twelve o'clock."

"I understand. I overslept."

"I know you overslept. Twelve-thirty." He jabbed his wristwatch. "Thirty minutes late. I should charge you another day."

"Thank you," I said, "for not."

"Hurry up and go."

"I will." I motioned for him to come closer. "You know a girl named Azal? She set you onto me?"

"Azal? Azal's a Persian name. I'm not Iranian."

"You never heard of SAVAK? You're not with them, right?"

"What are you talking about, SAVAK? What'd I just say? I'm not a goddamn Persian. You stupid fucker, I'm from Iraq. I should charge you two days, now."

"Sorry, sorry. It's just I have to be careful. These women, you know."

"Yeah, I know. But I'm not Persian. And there's no SAVAK now. There hasn't been a SAVAK for twenty fucking years. Those guys must be in wheelchairs. Why you talk about SAVAK?"

"Azal, see, she might have put them onto me."

"Crazy fucking Persians. There's no SAVAK. Don't worry about SAVAK. Worry about me."

"Okay."

"You're nuts. Stop doing drugs."

I closed the door and once again had to skip a shower. My skin was absorbing my clothes like they were Crackerjack tattoos. The hangover was sinking me, having torpedoed a bottle-lip-sized hole in my stern. If I just had money to spare, I'd drive to K-Mart, buy a shirt and jeans, to fool myself if no one else that I would feel better later.

Which gave me an idea.

I went to the office. The Iraqi slammed his pen on the desk. "Now what?"

"You need help around here?"

"Help what for?"

"I don't know. Anything."

"You need money? How bad you need money?"

"Bad as you hate Persians."

"You're broke? You Americans, falling apart one by one." He took out his wallet and counted bills. "You work under table. Clean every toilet. Nobody here now, all whores gone. Clean every toilet, bathroom floor, walls, sinks. Whole goddamn bathroom. Then you get the fifty bucks. I'll give you bucket and mop."

Soon, I was learning more than I ever cared to know about what people leave behind in motel bathrooms. I bet he had a crew of maids, at least one, maybe two, so he was doing me a favor, but it didn't feel like it when I dropped used rubbers in the trashcan.

It took three hours to clean all those bathrooms. There's no labor protection when under the table, not even a union of one. All this thanks to Rosie's financial wizardry, which I saluted by whistling spirituals of my own devise.

"All done?"

"Every single one."

"Good work. I know because I went back and checked a few. Not every one. I trust you. Here's your fifty bucks."

I took the money. "You just bought me some clothes."

"Good luck to you in your new clothes. And stay away from that woman. Persian women fucking crazy."

I walked toward my car. "Morning, Dapple."

Finishing that kind of job can work a person into a damn good mood. It sapped some of the juice from my blood. I re-swore the oath. I might have slipped, put my own two feet on the banana peel, but it was back to the other job, no monkey business. Next stop, Bakersfield, to see a Japanese speed freak who read comic books ninety pages per minute. Another sunny day, dreams drooping from my limbs like palm leaves. Five miles down the road, I fell asleep and into the rock tumbler of my mind.

Earthquake 3.0

Richter time is here again. Drum roll, please...
Sing of plots, connect dots, obey screenplays.
Is Daddy dead? Secrets give me the creeps.
Punch-drunk letters, hardboiled eggs: tough to crack.
"Here, Sir Paranoid: Seashells from Japan."
"From who, your king? Or emperors, I mean?"
Stomped words, my grapes, from Hollywood and Vine.
Shit, man, anything might be coming soon,
the shakiest John you ever did know,
underneath the earthquake, trapped in the crack.

Five

So I carried myself to Bakersfield, all the way thinking, "You want a mother, right? No, you don't want a mother. You just wanna know what you want." Would I find it in Bakersfield?

Lord, Bakersfield looked like home, and by that I mean I would rather have been any place but one place else. Saginaw was Bakersfield's sister city and I'd lived with her for more years than I cared to remember. These industrial zones contaminated my dreams, utilities and factories steeling in every direction, millions of thingamabobs and wobble springs, an infinity of Gary, Indiana.

It could only be guessed how Kerrie ended up here in the first place, and she wouldn't tell. I suspected child abuse, swinging parents, or some kidnaping incident. She liked it only because she loved alienation, and there could be nothing more alien than Kerrie in Bakersfield. She belonged in Manhattan, injecting ink into junky arms. But what Bakersfield offered was a multitude of meth labs cooking up Walmart cocaine on the outskirts of town, in trailers next to Joshua trees, over which birds must have felt supersonic as they soared through chemical residue.

In such a trailer she lived. Somehow, she had acquired the property, the trailer propped on real estate as worthless as land can get, at least until the day sand and mirrors become rare.

The last thing I passed was a state police post. I wondered if Kerrie ever worried about its proximity. I wondered if it still mattered.

With its satellite dish and aluminum sheen, the trailer should have been roving Mars. From the trash bin alone, I knew she hadn't left. Twenty empty boxes of Fruit loops and about as many milk containers were piled to capacity. She had another VW Bug, too, cockroaches that multiply before they're killed. If she lived to be a thousand, she would find one in operable condition, preferably sky blue with rusted hubcaps and a motor audible twenty miles away. As usual, there was a bumpersticker, but instead of think this or stop that, it stated, "GOD CAN WAIT: YOU CAN'T."

The screen door welcomed flies; I assumed I was also welcome, if wingless. She always left the door unlocked, never fearing burglars or dealers, rapists, killers. I did. I used to sleep tight against her because I knew that should a criminal arrive, Kerrie would protect me. If shined upon her rare REM, a flashlight would radiate her brain until it exploded, and the illuminator had better hit the bricks before the shit hit the fan. She was six feet tall with black hair to her waist, and she'd use that hair to strangle some-body if the situation demanded. To describe her as skin and bones would be an exaggeration in the wrong direction. Her bones were concealed weapons.

"Dang," she said. "I knew it."

"Knew what? And knew it how?"

"Nothing. Just come in."

She let me open the door myself. It was a surprise to see the place in order. There was a TV in the corner, a coffee table with nothing on it, a futon, one general issue halogen floor lamp, and—even I couldn't believe this one—a Persian cat hiding under the curtain. A woman I met later in my wandering, Chartrise, used to tell me there's a collective unconscious and something else, synchronicity, that sends us clues as to our destiny. But that Persian cat reminded me there's enough evidence in this world to sew a case shut on just about anything. License plate numbers, weather forecasts, the Dow Jones, they convince a person how the world's web is spun. But I looked at the cat and tried to remember: We are the spiders. We make the webs.

Kerrie stood in the kitchen. I sat on the couch.

"What, do you mean, you knew?"

"I don't want to get into it. I just know I'm being tested by something. Or somebody."

"You sent the letter, not me."

"The letter."

Not a question, I noted. "So you did send it?"

"No, I didn't send a letter."

I retrieved it from my pocket, a kid's homework assignment after a football game in the mud and a bath with the pants on. I stretched it using both hands. I wasn't about to let her touch it. She came near and read. Then she snatched the letter and shred it like paper maché.

"Juvenile bullshit."

"Juvenile delinquency," I shouted. "Vandalism."

"Calm down. Don't get angry with me."

How I hated adrenaline. "Let's think for a minute. Just sit with me on the couch."

"Don't touch me."

"I'm not touching anyone."

The cat watched me. Kerrie sat on the other end of the couch, arms crossed in a shield.

"What about e-mail?" I said. "You got a computer?"

"For God's sake, somebody else must have sent it. You probably sent it yourself when you were drunk."

"I don't drink anymore. Usually."

"Me, either. Or anything else. So I'd remember. That's the kind of thing somebody writes when they're wasted. Do I look wasted to you?"

"No." Even without the lamp, she bore a halogen glow.

"There's something wrong with you, John," she said. "I've prayed for you."

"Well, it didn't do any good."

"Have *you*?"

"Have I what?"

"Prayed?"

"Not in any way that doesn't include four-letter words."

"Jeez."

The cat loped toward me. I thought at first it must be Azal, with a little spraypaint can in its paw. It hopped on the couch and into my lap.

"She likes you," Kerrie said.

My body felt older, but Kerrie had regenerated in my absence. I sensed her rigidity giving way, legs stretching further and further from the couch until she was slumped in relaxation.

Back when we were together, she always sat forward, elbows on knees, alligator jaws clamped as she chewed her tongue and explained conspiracies that spider-veined from Washington to Berlin to Copenhagen to Rio de Janeiro to London to Cape Town to Riyadh and back to Washington. She had it all figured out, except the story kept digging deeper, as if she squatted behind a hedgehog's ass, pushing with all her might.

It wasn't a resort where I had met her but a mis-named hotel with a swimming pool. I guess that qualified in this crater. Back then, Kerrie was a hotel maid. She employed speed to her advantage, working twelve hour shifts.

One morning, she came into my room to clean while I was still sleeping, and she was halfway done when I awoke. She sat at the foot of the bed, on my foot. I jerked out from under her, but the landing gear was up, and she was flying too high to notice. She held herself, wings cracking in the velocity. She lay back and moaned, then slid next to me. I removed the "Do Not Disturb" sign from her hand and tossed it on the floor.

"I've been watching you," she said.

"Just sleep."

"They'll fire me."

"That's better than dying."

I got up and found the bottle in my luggage. I unwrapped the plastic glass she had left on the dresser and poured two shots of whiskey into it.

"Here."

I sat beside her. She could barely hold the cup, so I guided her hand with my palm.

"Medicine."

She gulped and kept it down. What she needed was Valium, but I hoped once the liquor grabbed, she would settle. It wasn't working, so I poured more.

"You need a doctor."

She made it through another shot. She sat up. I knew right where she was: The second she started feeling better, she would hit the runway again, Phoenix in California.

"No," I said, helping her back. I lay beside her and brought her toward me.

"I've been studying you. You seem lonely."

"I've got my own problem. You just drank it."

"I know. The waste basket's always full of bottles. Will you sneak me out? They'll come looking for me."

"You sleep. I've got the room for another day. We'll get you out of here later."

I found the "Do Not Disturb" sign, opened the door and hung the tag on the handle. I looked both directions and pushed her cart to the end of the hall. Then I came back and got in bed beside her. She slept while I wondered exactly where we were headed.

Four hours later, I found out: an Airstream trailer so full of comic books that the thing practically leaked ink. She slept for a day. I read the comic books and drank. By the time she awoke, I had passed out. And that was the way we would spend our relationship.

"Funny," she said now, "the way you look mostly white. You couldn't even guess from looking at your eyes. They're not really Asian. It's a flaw, isn't it? But a pretty flaw. Still, you're a mess."

"I'm trying to iron things out. But every morning, I wake up wrinkled again."

"You have to sleep in your skin."

It was getting dark outside. Soon, I would have to ask whether I could spend the night.

"So what's with the bumpersticker?" I said.

"Uh-uh."

"Must mean something."

"I'm not talking about it with you. It's not about higher powers and blah blah blah. It's not that. But you'll laugh anyway."

"I'm just curious."

"I don't want to say." She went to the kitchen and started with the coffee. I think she knew I was about to touch her hand. "You're totally lost," she said, setting the filter in the tray and filling the coffeemaker with bottled water.

"You can say anything you like. I won't laugh. What do I know?

"Okay, then, this is the story. That VW bug out there? It was the only one I could afford when I bought it. I didn't even kick the tires or take it for a test drive. I just bought it.

"Then, when I got it home, I sat on the stoop. It was only a couple of weeks after I'd quit meth. I still felt completely off-kilter, separated, and everything looked like it does through 3-D glasses. I wondered if it would ever end, that maybe I'd done permanent brain damage, messed up my vision or my cortex or something. And I started thinking, 'Okay, Kerrie, if this is how it's going to be, and you're going to be coming off it forever, then why not keep doing it? What's the point of not doing it when you feel depressed and paranoid anyway?'

"That's when I saw the bumpersticker. And when I saw it, it was like I was being personally asked a question by God right there in the desert. But while I was being asked, there was a succubus from one of my comic books sitting on the next step down, telling me to do more meth.

"But I felt a little better. I felt that something might take care of me, like a dad from the sixties telling his kid, 'Speed kills.' Any other day, I would have found an old razor blade and scraped the sticker off. But I decided to leave it in place. One day, somebody in the same condition might drive behind me, and they'd see the question. Maybe it would make them feel a little better and get them through a few hours. That's all it is.

"Now it's my turn," she continued. "*You're* married?"

The question made me realize I hadn't been thinking of Rosie at all.

"More like indentured."

"Not gonna last?"

"Ever been in a relationship so fucked up it's not even worth explaining?"

"All of them."

Kerrie produced a pack of imported cigarettes from her shirt pocket. She extracted one and lit it with precision. She smoked it slowly, making it last.

"What's your wife like?"

"A bull, and I'm no matador. I get the horns every time. Forget her. Let's go out on the stoop."

Her cigarette seemed to last half an hour. The clock slurred, drunk on this odd moment. I nodded in and out and the desert rocks seemed to divide and multiply. Soon, we were on the moon, with another moon above us. The coyotes went after cats, but Azal was safe inside the trailer.

"Is that a menthol cigarette?"

"Yeah. Why?"

"Nothing. You don't have gospel records, do you?"

"Nope."

"A friend named Jesus?"

"What are you getting at?"

"Just making sure things stay random."

"They're not."

I looked at the bumpersticker but experienced no revelation. I saw a blur of motion, the whiz of pre-decision. I mean I began to understand this mission was dividing into itself, into me. The math was getting even more complicated, beyond calculation. Was I backtracking for some true love, the letter my excuse to go looking? No, I didn't love Kerrie. I admired but didn't love her. There was no heat on the stoop. The closeness we felt was warm but sexless. We were brother and sister now. Sex was possible, true, but against some natural law. We weren't going back there, not there. It was a painting, impressionistic: Humans on Stoop, Contemplating. Dots and dots and dots. It would take ten thousand ellipses to describe it, but something would be left out, the something I always sensed but couldn't touch.

"Did you ever figure it all out?" I said.

"Figure what out?"

"Your conspiracy."

"I quit playing that game. This is better, don't you think, at the edges, standing back? A respectful distance. Like the distance we're keeping from each other."

"I don't know."

"I do. I'm looking at your eyes, and I know you need a place to sleep. I know you don't want to ask because you'll think I'll say no, worried I'll think you're trying to sleep with me. So, you can sleep with me. No, not that way. Just beside me. That's close enough, isn't it?"

Finale

We went to bed. Azal slept beside us. I mean the cat. It was the closest to a three-way I ever had.

The next morning, we drank the coffee she had made the night before. Neither of us had undressed for bed. That would not have been staying at the edges, nor respectful to the law that said, "Not tonight. Never again."

I was wrinkled. We both were. But I realized something about getting older, that there's a camaraderie in it once somebody you haven't seen in years stops laughing at your gut and yellow-belly hairline.

We drank the coffee. The breeze from the window said, "Don't leave," but the law said, "Leave soon."

I looked for a washer and dryer but the trailer lacked both. What a pleasure clean clothes had become now that I never had them. I always had yesterday on my back.

"I've got something for you," she said.

Kerrie went to the kitchen cabinets and stood on her toes. From the top shelf, behind a bag of sugar, slumped a lunch sack. She brought it to the table and dropped it in my hands. I opened the bag and looked inside. A Caesar salad of cash.

She said, "I started selling meth after you left, to make ends meet—the end of the straw and the end of my nose. That's when it got really bad, because I always had a stash. I never ran out, so I never stopped. Teenagers coming here all hours of the night, fratboys. I hate those little shits. In fifty years, you're gonna see eighty-year-olds riding around in their Lincolns, slumped down in the seat, one arm slung across the steering wheel, a backwards AARP baseball hat on their heads. They still come around once in a while. I say, 'Get lost.' I won't spend that pile of money. But you can."

If I had put the money in my wallet, my ass would have been bigger than Rosie's. I'd have to stash the bag and convert it to bigger bills at the bank.

We finished our coffee. We were still dream-cooked, sun warming us. I was feeling less and less law-abiding, but the law didn't care how I felt.

"I should—"

"Yeah," she said. "Will you do one thing? Quit looking."

"I can't. I have to know."

"You're writing this."

"What, the letters?"

"The whole story, dummy."

"You tore up the first page last night. But I've got it memorized."

"Un-memorize it. Over the last years, I've made a religious survey, but none of them quite took. I still learned a few things. You know what the Koran says? 'Ask not about things that, if made plain to you, may cause you trouble.'"

I headed for the door and said, "I'll try to remember that."

"You won't."

She kissed my cheek and went inside. I looked at the bumpersticker. Nothing. When I got into my car, I stashed the bag of money under the seat. I was happy not to see "ASSHOLE" on the hood, and though my only new clue was that Kerrie hadn't sent the letter, my heart felt half-repaired. I had no instinct to cry. Memories of Rosie delivered no blows. Even my body felt better. I bore a halogen glow, which lasted ten seconds, until I pulled the reins on Dapple and slammed into the car behind me.

"What the shit?" I shouted, jumping out of the car.

"You tell me," the driver said. He was one of those kids Kerrie had described.

"You didn't see me sitting there?" I said.

"I saw you sitting there picking your ass. How was I supposed to know you were gonna back up?"

"Because that's what people sitting in driveways do."

"Bullshit. Is Kerrie here?"

101

Finale

He tipped his hat back, revealing pot seeds for eyes. He must have longed for something that moved faster, that would make him feel like Jack on the Beanstalk.

"Why?" he said. "You her old man?"

"She's not selling anymore. She's cleaned up."

"That's not what I heard."

"Find another crockpot because this one stopped cooking. There's labs all over the place, genius."

He scratched a pimple on his nose. "I'm thinking about kicking your ass."

I walked away. He opened his door, knocking me off balance. Then he grabbed my shoulder and tried to spin me, but I was too heavy for him.

Now Kerrie was on the stoop.

"Get inside," I said.

"I'm calling the cops."

"You hear that? She's calling the cops."

"All right, asshole," the kid said. "I'm leaving."

He backed out and kept backing up, probably reversing all the way to mom's house so he wouldn't get lost.

"It's all right," I yelled to Kerrie.

I got in my car and took off. Things had ended between us as well they could, and I didn't want one wrong word or gesture scratching out the memory and leaving another blemish.

Back to the main road. But when I looked in the mirror, that kid was behind me, arm extended out the window at a ninety-degree angle, waving hello in a most unfriendly fashion.

The son of a bitch was trying to ram me. I gave the car gas but couldn't shake him. I took the turn toward town as hard as I could, but he stayed an inch off my bumper with one hand on the wheel, the other still signaling his displeasure.

"Come on, Dapple."

We sailed on a straightaway now. I had one idea and aimed straight for it. The kid must have slammed the pedal because at mid-burst his car hit mine, which slid to the right. At the instant of my trying to recall whether I should turn the wheel with or against the spin, I guessed correctly. Physics straightened the car and I shot down a hill, gaining space. Then, just as he was about to catch up, I yanked the wheel all the way to the right and bounded into the police station at forty-five miles an hour, the kid following me for one-thirtieth of a second before realizing where I was going and then swerving back onto the main road.

Now a cop three inches from the hood of my car said, "What—the—fuck?"

"Did you see that guy? The guy who just went a hundred miles an hour past this station?"

"Step out, please."

It seemed that I, like Kerrie, was being tested, only I couldn't believe in that kind of thing. It had to be biology, nature against me, that I wasn't supposed to multiply. I had no problem with that. Neither did anyone else.

"Did it occur to you," the cop said, "that speeding into a police station is a bad idea?"

"I was being chased."

"By whom?"

"A guy trying to buy drugs from my ex-girlfriend."

As soon as I said it, I knew I had to be the dumbest guy in Bakersfield, and there was plenty of competition for the ribbon.

"You can probably guess," he said, "what I'm going to ask next."

"Kerrie Katsumata."

"I know that name."

"But she doesn't sell anymore. She doesn't even use."

"I know that, too. At least I thought I did."

He motioned me out of his way and searched the car.

"What about you?" he said. "You use? Why the hell's somebody chasing you?"

"An incident in Kerrie's driveway. I backed into him."

"Drinking?"

"Not yet."

I heard the bag crackle before I saw it in his hand. "And what's this?"

"Bag of money."

"Drug money?"

"Just money."

"I don't think so. Let's go inside."

I went into the administrative light, fluorescence illuminating the office as if this were bureaucratic heaven. We sat in cubicle 12B. I explained the money. He registered the evidence.

"She doesn't sell," I said. "She gave it to me. That's my money."

"Has it crossed your mind that this could be our drug buy money?"

Now they had me on a list. I added them to my own list: Dennis; SAVAK; a kid with a backwards baseball cap; the state police; Rosie; Mary; Azal; and, when the cops showed up at her place, Kerrie.

I said, "I suppose you're going to her trailer later?"

He looked at me, shook his head. "Not later; they're already there. She just called us. What about this kid? Got a name?

"I don't know the name. Maybe Kerrie does."

"License number?"

"Never saw the plate."

"Car description?"

"I don't know about cars. It was small and green."

"Jesus."

He dumped the bag of money and counted.

"That's two thousand, two hundred, twenty-three dollars," he said. "Interesting: lots of twos. You know what day this is?"

"Tuesday?"

"Second day of the week." He licked his finger and counted off two hundred bucks, handing it to me. "That's a deposit. You can come back and get the rest if we clear it. Or Kerrie can pick it up."

"And when—"

"Shhh. The next question costs the two hundred dollars I shouldn't have slipped you in the first place."

I drove half a mile and parked on a road, car aimed at the sun. Bees landed on the hood. They wanted inside, so I left the air conditioning running, the engine working on the money one drop of gas at a time. Evidence of Kerrie's plot, courtesy of Saudi Arabia, exhaled into the American desert halfway across the world.

My conscience told me I should go back to her, but it was fight or flight, and two addicts are not stronger than one. *Boom* went my cortex, splattering fear. In that fear, I imagined bird-fish flying above, telling me, "Scram, boy, scram." Are cowardice and bravery merely chemical reactions? If so, I needed a transfusion, for I was on the run again. My conscience wasn't good for much besides telling me to do what it already knew I wouldn't.

Then a real bird landed next to the bees, a Biblical sign, some might have said. I honked the horn.

"Fuck off."

I wondered if I shouldn't drive home. But the thought of Rosie made me woozy, as if she could belt me from all these miles beyond her hand.

The bird returned. I honked ten times before it flapped away. A few of the bees melted on the hood, too exhausted to zoom away before their stingers stuck.

I needed something. All I had was this mission. Without it, there was only back there, but a home in chaos is no home and has no welcome mat. It becomes a hospital. I would thank the staff for my recovery, but I couldn't wait to leave. "Goodbye, Nurse Rosie. I am Ulysses, not ready to rust, though my knowledge sinks by the second."

I drove to the "resort" where I had met Kerrie. I no longer had my card—tearing it up had been the prenupt Rosie demanded—so I paid for the night. Once inside the room, I saw Kerrie on the bed. And then she faded.

I plugged in the laptop until it had enough juice to glow. There was a single message, this one from FLUSHINGJOHNTHOMAS: "Have you found me yet? I won't tell. Why don't you go home, so I can find you? That would be easier for both of us. And here's something else: If you don't find me soon, I'll kill myself and pin it on you. Don't ask how. I know how. I've got your fingerprints all over the place."

Oh. Uh-oh.

Whoever it was knew I'd left home. She knew I was looking for her. That meant she might be one of the women I'd already visited, but I couldn't be sure. Mary didn't seem a logical choice, unless she had left that day to email me from some other location, the egg box a ruse. But then there was Jesus, who knew all about the box. Kerrie was convinced she had found redemption in a bumpersticker, and she had been kind to me, plus we had not engaged in what natural law considered incest. That left Azal. And, I supposed, Dennis the Menace and SAVAK could not be ruled out.

I couldn't go home. Something was happening. And that, I still believed, was better than nothing. But as soon as I hit the mattress, I felt a 4.0 coming, coming.

Earthquake 4.0

We must climb these webs we spin: we spiders.

Reached the moon but still stuck with desert words.

Reject revisions of dead spells, ignore

jet-exhaust clues, supersonic secrets.

Is the crack man-made? I'm too old for this.

The hour is now: These are your orders.

Ulysses, I admire your last mission,

but this is my enlistment, my tour.

Paris, Berlin: the expatriate's list.

Build internment camps for all Persian cats,

just in case. You never know. Can't be sure.

Sleeping in a flying trailer, I see

3-D beanstalks, bird-fish. Dream cooked, I am.

Sleep, matador, sleep. Please do not disturb.

Four

Never forget to leave the "Do Not Disturb" sign on the door. They knock and open the door. When they see you're still in bed, they mutter, "Goddamn it" because they want to clean *now*. But I was thinking maybe the world's most supernaturally-gifted maid would open that door. She would take my palm and say: "I know what's wrong with you. It's right here in your palm."

Instead, I spun out of the autumn leaves of hotel bedspreads and walked to the balcony. I conjured a mental map of California and how far it was to Fresno, my next stop. I wondered if I would ever leave the Golden State. Why not go to Florida and swim to Cuba? Or Michigan and hop a bridge to Canada? Or Vietnam and see if I could locate a pair of idols with needled-pocked veins under their wood skins? I could slip a joker in the deck and see what fanned out, or shave an edge off the die and throw it with a certain snap of the fingers, or tape a tail to a tail and watch it come up heads every time. I could do a lot of things, but my choices seemed unlimited and, therefore, worthless. Then reason narrowed them, whittled them to almost nothing, less than toothpicks and easy to break. Still worthless.

Now suicide, or murder in some undefined degree, might be added to my future rap sheet. Killing by tardiness, with the clocks to prove it. Was that a chargeable offense?

I still felt better, cleansed of hangover. I inhaled today's oxygen, not yesterday's ethanol. No shotgun nerves, no internal jigsaw. I was not eclipsed by last night's moon but brightened by this morning's sun. I remembered when it was the other way around. Abstaining had been an accomplishment and could not be taken from me. Whenever I succumbed to the bloodlust, I remembered I had fought many wars and would fight again. The final outcome of these battles would be determined by the will and my fucked up napalm genes. I was shipped into this world with a ready-made plot. I could affect the outcome to an extent, but time's sponge must eventually absorb me. I would learn this, but I hadn't learned it yet: There was choice, and there was no choice.

I decided to dump the rest of Kerrie's money bag, not out of frivolousness but a kind of tribute. Surprise money should be spent on surprises, just as minimum wages must go to electric companies and landlords.

I ordered room service. I had a breakfast big as Rosie would have prepared, subtracting the whack. It was twenty times what a hundred diners in Bakersfield would charge and worth it, fifteen bucks for the food, fifteen for the repose.

After breakfast, I stretched on the bed and watched TV. I called room service again and had my clothes taken to the laundry. I finished my Elmore Leonard novel. I replaced his sentences with mine and began to wonder: just maybe...

I took a shower. I avoided the mirror because I was in good spirits, and there was little in my reflection to buoy them. I would never be a porn star, despite a name that held some promise in that direction; misdirection, actually, as I've never purposefully peeked in locker rooms but had witnessed enough to know.

When the clothes finally arrived from the laundry, I dressed. I added Elmore Leonard's book to the Bible drawer, my version of Kerrie's bumpersticker. Insomniacs would thank heaven for something besides the Gideon.

Back to Dapple, my poor donkey of a car. The thing seemed to look at me and moan when I turned the key. It all but brayed. It wanted no destination. I didn't kick it but yanked the reins. We rolled, both dented by our adventures.

With Fresno two hours ahead, we headed back to the highway, Dapple and me. If only I had a Sancho to bind my wounds. Ten minutes later, I had no Dapple, either.

It died on the freeway entrance ramp, with a boom and a Looney Tunes' puff of smoke. Another engine, gone. No need for autopsy; I knew the signs and walked away. I've never been one to remember oil changes. The car's last words would have been, "Can't you at least have me towed to the graveyard?"

"You heard what I said about bones."

I walked the five miles back to town. I asked around, and somebody pointed me to the bus station, where I bought a ticket on a deal good for a month to and from anywhere in California. That was the last of the money.

The bus was filled with senior citizens on the way to some state fair in Fresno. I sat next to a guy who had cancer. I learned all about chemotherapy, subliminally, because I was thinking of Aquamarine, named by a new-aged mother with bottle-blond for each lock, one percent Indian for stock and ninety-nine WASP for barrel. Her daughter, saddled by the name, had somehow lassoed everyone into calling her Marnie, a variation on Marine, and the alphabet trick worked. I mean she really was a Marnie, a cute American girl, not yet woman despite her legal age, who would never be mistaken for her mothership, just an average gal and not the usual type to grace my semi-existence.

We met at the Big Boy restaurant where she served as hostess. I had stopped there just after leaving Kerrie the first time years before, stranding her wrecked as Dapple. I hadn't even booked a resort when we found something in common. The register was down, so we chatted while I waited to pay.

She said her name was Aquamarine, and the other kids called her Marine until the day she explained her father had been a Marine killed in Vietnam. Lie. So the kids asked what she wanted to be called. She said,

"Hold it," then went to the public library and found a name-your-baby book. She saw "Marnie" and knew. She later made it legal at City Hall, but her mother still insisted upon Aquamarine. The mothership brought the daughter weekly bags of crystals and therapeutic scents instead of Campbell's soup and Ramon noodles.

That night, we had take-out, but I was bagged from a day recovering at the bar. I told Marnie all about Kerrie. Marnie took me home. I was her pet for a day and then she let me sleep in her bed. We had the chemistry of opposites, for Marnie would never leave Fresno. Too content with a hostess job, she would never be called to the path of the pathless.

"I get planters warts from the chemo," the man beside me said.

I tried to listen the rest of the way. Some people can handle absolutely anything, violation by medical instruments, scanners and rayguns, needles and prods, leeching and tubing. I had another hour of his dissertation to go and at the end of it said, "Good luck to you." That satisfied him. Perhaps he knew most people wanted to talk about anything but his condition, and since I hadn't talked at all, he assumed I had been an exception.

"You're a good boy, son."

Son? Sun?

I had to walk to Marnie's place, another three miles. I wandered as if I were still twelve and riding my bike, pretending I would end up somewhere better. Back then, I had to return home, where Mother constantly corrected the way I stood, how I held a spoon, everything but the way I pissed, and probably even that if I hadn't have locked the door behind me.

I remembered the way to Marnie's apartment. Soon I came to a complex of cheap condos, a neighborhood for the money-challenged. Most of the tenants were single mothers and fathers bounced from divorce court. It was a perfect mating grounds for the shattered. One week I would see a guy walking into one apartment and the next week another, and so on. In a way, it was the perfect place for me, where people roamed without leaving Rome. More efficient.

I knocked, but there was no answer. Then a woman and her young daughter approached.

"Marnie still live here?"

"Nope. Marnie left a month ago. Don't know where she went. Just upped and disappeared."

There were two possibilities; as mentioned, Marnie would not have left Fresno. She was either at the Big Boy or had been career-propelled to Applebees, or she was at home with her mother, Poke-and-Haunt-Us.

So I went to the mothership's house, one mile away. It wouldn't be hard to find, so many crystals hanging in the windows that astronauts could probably spot the sparkle from space. But when I crossed the distance, I saw no gem-stone glow. There was only another tract house, just like the rest. It occurred to me that America had long been in the process of trying to make every place resemble every other place until one needn't go anywhere to be everywhere.

When I knocked, the mothership opened the door. She was no longer semi-Indian. Now she was semi-African. She wore a multicultural garbage bag of garb and a hat that capped the ceiling. She had microwaved herself the color of oranges. She had a weird peace about her, a lobotomized song of content. Masks hung on the walls. Wooden giraffes and tigers and elephants tried to stalk the carpet, but they were paralyzed, zooed by stucco.

"You for Aquamarine?" she said. "Come in, my dear."

I sat on a bench and felt this retail Africa pinch my brain. She brought me a cup of tea steaming with cinnamon scent.

"She home soon."

"That accent: You've been to Africa?"

"Oh, indeed. I went with my group from the college extension class. Ended up staying a year. My life changed."

"And what about Marnie?"

"Marnie?"

"Aquamarine."

"Akilah, you mean. One who reasons. Reasons too much. Settling, always settling. I wish she would explore the world."

"So what do I call you?"

"Deka. One who pleases."

The way she looked at me... Long ago, Deka—the mothership—liked to touch my hand when she laughed, and sometimes she would squeeze, and occasionally she would somehow stroke the hair on my arms until chills ran from limb to groin. Despite my efforts, I would find myself eroticized. This would happen right in front of Marnie, who would send smoke signals of distress.

"Why you here, child?"

"I came to find your daughter. I've got to talk to her."

"You stayed away so long. I miss you."

Despite her fraudulent accent and tan, I was starting to believe she really was African. Such strange smells permeated the apartment. I waited for some tribal rite, expecting that soon she would stretch my neck to giraffe-proportions or bore half-dollar holes in my lobes.

"She home in two hours. I prepare you welcome gift."

She went to the bedroom and returned with a necklace. Unless I was mistaken, at the center of the medallion shined something that for once was not zirconia.

"Very valuable. I met a man involved in diamond trade. He give me such things. I cannot use them *all*! Besides, they remind me of home. I should go back. Yes, I will go back. But for now, I give you this."

She stood behind me, fingers tracing along my neck—slowly, gently—before finally clasping the necklace. After that, they found their way to my chest. The mothership orbited until she was all around me, Africa absorbing America.

Finale

"Ah," she said, thrusting in a manner I could not refuse. "Two hours, we have. Then we dress. Akilah will know nothing."

We went to the bedroom. She undressed me. She looked at me and then pulled me back. She wasn't difficult to undress, as there was nothing underneath the silk. She was the orange light, but the red spot was my mind—or Marnie's. And blue? The blues are for the last time with the woman before, better than the sadness of any current moment.

"You know what to do, still."

"What do you mean, still?"

"You do not bring much, but you bring it often."

We moved faster and faster, her continent joining mine, geography's progress reversed. And after I had been consumed, she said, "We dress now. Some time she arrive early. Hurry, hurry."

I went to the bathroom and tried to re-Americanize myself. But no matter how much water I splashed, my hair remained bed-matted and I still smelled of foreign intimacies.

"Come, come," she called from the zoo.

Marnie was home. I came out of the bathroom and stood in that living room with the expression of a village idiot.

"What," Marnie said, "are you doing here?"

"I just—"

"He misses you, my dear," the mothership said. "He's our guest."

"Unwanted guest."

"But Akilah, my love, this is no way to talk."

"Marnie: My name is Marnie."

"Oh," the mothership said, laughing, "that's just a nickname."

So there we stood, me in my K-Mart clothes, Marnie in her Big Boy uniform, Deka in her silks. I could hear Marnie's brain clicking like a slot machine.

"Leave us alone, Mother."

"I go to bedroom."

"No, please go altogether. Go to the store. Buy some yam mush and ground millet, some fritters and batters, a box of starch, greens for steaming, a melon, some peanuts. Let's have a feast."

"Now you talk, Akilah."

"An African feast. Ha!"

"I go now."

"Please hurry. Our unwanted guest is starving, obviously."

Deka found her purse, winked at me and left.

The door closed.

Marnie said, "Did you just fuck my mother?"

"What kind of thing is that to ask?"

"Wasn't that why you left the first time, because she kept humming around you? I believe it was Billie Holiday. Maybe you tried to resist, but I wasn't home just now, so as usual it wouldn't have mattered, would it?"

"Jeez, Marnie." Kerrie speaking through me, now. Correction: "Jesus Christ."

"So why are you here? Why Fresno? Not that I'm surprised."

She went to her room, changing out of her uniform, but her voice was loud and clear.

"Why wouldn't you be surprised I'm here?"

"Mother contacted African spirits? How should I know? And why should I tell you? I just know. And I know you're married, too. You just couldn't stand staying in one place, could you?"

She returned wearing a pastel sweater and khaki pants and penny loafers, the quintessential American girl—woman, but still, girl. The picture of practicality, a childless soccer mom. One with no mothership connection.

"Had to start wandering, but you're not looking for anything, are you? Quite the opposite. Did you ever notice your women stay in one place? Plenty of people search without leaving home. But you go here, there, everywhere, never finding anything new. You're running. Like my mother."

I kissed her. It must have been some rare extra-male part of me that took me to her lips. I wanted to get right inside the feminine plot, burrow my way into the tree of their sexuality: seed; root; branch; leaf. And, yes, to have mother and daughter both, within a span of minutes, would be something, though I had never been a notch collector nor ring counter.

I felt her give way for a second, but then her mouth closed and she pushed me back.

"Not so fast."

"Sorry—I don't know what I'm doing."

"The first thing you're doing is taking a shower."

"You think I really—"

"Just stop. Mother goes to bed early. I might sleep with you. But first I want to know why you think—what you're doing here."

I reached for the letter, then remembered it was gone. "I have no proof now, but someone sent a letter and some emails, too. Not very nice messages. They could have only come from out of the past, to haunt me. First they threatened murder, then suicide, only suicide as murder, by me, because—because—"

"Halt. You know why I work at Big Boy? Because I like the world the way it is, even the ugly parts, even the polyester uniforms and the old folks who come for the buffet. I like cheap cars and paying the bills on time. What I don't like are mothers who think they'll find themselves in Africa and come back looking like Pier One refugees. I don't care too much for wanderers, either, drifters and convicts, all you losers. Wherever you go, yeah. They're running to stop from going crazy. How'd you stay in one place for so long without going crazy? Or did you go crazy? It sounds like you did. Murder, suicide, murder. Why'd you leave your wife if you're so scared?"

116

"'Cause she's a one-woman road crew busting up my freeway."

"Maybe you need more concrete."

"I'm on the road again."

I sat at the "dining room" table, situated in the middle of the living room. Marnie lay on the couch and crossed her skinny legs, shopworn, bruised and dented from food-service chaos. She sighed, probably hoping her breath would sail me to the Pacific. Perhaps I'd find my suitcase, ride it like a raft to a Polynesian island. I'd reclaim my innocence in banana-ripe paradise, get it on with pygmies, shoot coconuts through hoops and swing from vines, hoping Gilligan fucked up the signal when a rescue plane piloted by Rosie flew overhead, the plane barely maintaining altitude from the cursing load within. I pondered Marnie's cliche, that wherever I went, et cetera, but it could also be argued that wherever Marnie was, there she was, and she hadn't seen much in the process besides fish and chips and triple burgers, stacks of pancakes and sausage links, and a steady stream of people ready to leap like salmon into death with a fork in one hand and a Big Boy tab in the other.

"You got any jobs at that restaurant?"

"You? Don't make me laugh."

"I need a car and some money. On the bus trip here, I learned more about cancer than I care to know."

"That necklace you're wearing is worth two thousand bucks. You must be a pretty good john, John. How many more girls are there?"

"Three to go. But Dapple broke down in Bakersfield. My car, I mean."

"I'll buy the necklace from you for fifteen hundred. How's that? My dad's probably dumb enough to buy it. He already bought it once with the alimony."

"Know anybody with a thousand-dollar car?"

"Wait a minute," she said, sitting up. "How do you know it wasn't me that sent the letter?"

"My gut says so."

"Yeah? Well, I like you, too, only I don't like you so much for screwing my mother. You sure you even care who sent that letter?"

"You mean I'm looking for something else?"

She shrugged. Then came a stomping and a rattling.

"Shit," Marnie said, "there she is. She can't cook. I wouldn't eat, if I were you."

We talked about Africa as Deka prepared something that smelled like Dapple's exhaust. Marnie sighed at each description of ceremony and ritual, of nights under stars with snakes wrapped around trees and rhinos on the prowl, of floppy-eared elephants who knew they were modern slaves waiting for P.T. Barnum's boats to arrive alongside the coast, of diamond mine shenanigans in which some seduced middleman supplied this traveler with lifted jewels, of ghosts in the bush and hallucinatory concoctions, of sex with men whose ears drooped to their shoulders, of dance lessons and the urban sprawl of the global economy. And after that, we ate something that tasted of punishment. I would not drink the potion put before me, but Marnie and Deka did, and soon they were drunk, heaving eyeshot spears across the table.

Finally, Deka said, "I'm going to bed, and you two can do whatever it is you're going to do—as if I didn't know. Keep the noise down. No howling, you hear me?"

In a moment, we fell on the couch, but Marnie was soon asleep, slumbering and lumbering. In the other room, her mother seemed to issue earthquake alerts. The apartment sounded like a 747 on liftoff. I was thinking any number of things but mostly that it was good I didn't sleep with Marnie, that these situations were part of the problem, set in motion by I don't know what, perhaps an instinct for the opposite of self-preservation or a Johnny Appleseed inclination to populate the world with wanderers. I realized how careless I had been, never taking precautions for all the disease in the world, not to mention those breaststroking fish of mine that lunged for the female form in the hopes of spawning strange new life forms. What the hell kind of offspring would I create, a Crayola zebra running in eight directions at once? Giraffes given to sipping from pools of liquor and attracting overly sympathetic females? Could I never plan for consequence, only react, shuffle, tapdance, skedaddle from one asinine adventure to the next? Would I never march in a straight line, only zigzag, like Gomer Pyle on goofballs, always headed to the wrong war? "Not Korea, stupid: Vietnam." And either way, wars that were over, fought, treatied into history books?

Father? Mother? Where were they to explain my birth? Why was I dropped in the lap of a sociopath who knew not the full variety of genital nicknames? And where did they go? Were they in the jungle somewhere, running deep through azure Joseph Conrad dreams? Or working at a Walmart and heading out for pizza on big occasions? Did they ever wonder what became of me? Or was I to them erased, smeared lead scribbles on earth's Etch-a-Sketch?

Were these the questions for which I sought the answers, or were they ancillary? This quest, this jousting with my sex history, poking holes in the fabric of my biography when not poking other holes, was it letting light through the gaps? And was it blinding me to myself until I wandered straight out of my body and into some airy sphere where I would become atoms and protons, my figure visible only in the patterns of dust seen at certain slants of sunlight?

"Teeny meanie," Marnie mumbled. "Iddy biddy. Ummmm. It's okay. I don't mind." She kicked my hip. She danced the goddamn Charleston, flip-flopping. "Go easy on the yoo-ya, girl....boy. Maga mashanini. Deka? Looks cut up, don't it? Splice and dice. You and he, Karma Suture."

She started laughing, the nutty laugh of sleep talkers, shorn of all pretense, sarcastic babble fueled by tips from the subconscious. I could not decipher. She, too, might as well have just come back from Africa, complete with cluck-cluck language and potions galore.

I moved to the floor and briefly fell asleep to key revelations. But the sleep was like a broken film reel, flickering, stammering, stopping, starting, until it flew off the spool. I woke up drenched three times. The next day would have the hallucinatory edge that comes with lack of sleep, the world inflated by REM indigestion. I'd done LSD once or twice, the wrong drug for alcoholics. We prefer comforters and easy dreams, not beds of nails and Yoga realizations. But the drug had burrowed into my brain and revealed its presence whenever I failed to sleep long enough.

Hours and hours later, Marnie awoke. One person sleeps as if charmed and the other cursed, then they share the time that follows as if there's no difference in their perception. How is it one man stands at a bus stop while another cruises past in a Cadillac, and in the intersection of their viewpoints time and space do not collapse from the absolute lack of agreement about their nature?

"I'd like to get out of here," I said, "before your mother awakes."

"Her? She's dreaming National Geographic. She won't be done for a long time."

"I'd like to sell that necklace soon. I should be going. I'm getting close to the end. Unless, that is, you really did send the letter?"

"No, John, I didn't send it. I'm not in eighth grade. I work ten hour shifts and in between try to keep my mother from deciding India might be better, or Timbuktu, anywhere but Fresno. I guess I should encourage her because, frankly, I can't stand her. But she—"

"She *is* your mother."

"You've never felt that way?"

"Which mother?"

"The one you know."

"She doesn't count. Calls me the Wanderer for a joke."

"Yet you can't wait to hop right in that car and ride around the world?"

"I've got no fists of iron. And I'm definitely not as happy as a clown."

"But you are a clown. So what if you find out who sent some letter? By now, she's come to her senses. If someone wanted to kill you, you'd be dead by now. How hard would it be to kill you? You've done half the job."

The room was giving me the jimjams. Was I trying to find myself or lose that self altogether? Did the jabs, the well-meant advice, the comments that we should lose or gain weight, try short or long hair, loosen up or keep a lid on it, not care what others believe or spend more time worrying what others think, cause such dislocation? "Don't stand with your hands on your hips and for Christ's sake, I drilled a hole in the bathroom door and saw for myself that you piss sitting down. It's your father's fault, him or the Chink. Never saw you throw a football, just wandering around on that bike of yours, taking the wayward path. Won't even kick a soccer ball. One day, John, you'll end up in a soup kitchen with all the other wanderers, who discover on admittance that misfits don't fit together, all the missing puzzle pieces in one shitty room, except they belong to different puzzles. Some will knife each other while the preacher beats the meat in the refectory. Some will take the short walk to the next institution. Some will finally learn to defend themselves like men by boxing themselves on city streets. They mutter in secret tongues because they've fallen out of the common language. You're not with the program and we've issued a dishonorable discharge. We fight wars we understand no better than anyone else but accept them as our common if unwanted lot, while you and your father watch the rain in jungles of your own making, where even the snakes and insects are invented." Well, Mother never said all that, but she might as well have.

"What in the world are you thinking about?" Marnie said.

"I need to leave. I've got to go."

"I don't have that much money. I can give you some; I cashed my check on the way home."

"How much?"

121

Finale

"Five hundred."

"Then you'll what, sell the necklace?"

"I'll give it to my father. He can sell it. He deserves it. I'd like to sell everything she brought back with her. I'd sell her bones and skin, too. I doubt anybody would pay much for the brain."

Worlds collapsed, continents converged, faultlines quaked. Panic attack? But such description obscures the fact the world becomes so thoroughly projected that the flickering images form a continuous stream, indistinguishable from what plays beyond the screen, the movie in which everyone else participates. The theater owner—who, me?—holds a gun to the back of the head: "You watch this one, see? No changing films, understand? You watch. I leave now." Voice of SAVAK. Orders in the night. And laughable to anyone else, this paranoia operating like jealousy. "You think I'm sleeping with him?" But the laughter becomes something else, further proof, evidence of the most subtle plots, deception finery, spookcraft. It's like a Chinese fingercuff: The harder you pull, the more stuck you find yourself, and the harder the prankster laughs.

"What is wrong with you?"

"Can you drive me somewhere?"

"Of course. Where to?"

I told her. She laughed. But I couldn't ride the Cancer Express again, the Tumor Trails. I couldn't stand those wheels, nor could I afford four of my own. But I could afford two.

We found a dealership. The dealer was attentive: We were the only ones in the store. He wanted to show me every model invented since 1963.

"Fuck it," I said, "give me the best you've got for five hundred bucks. I don't give a shit if it's pink with tassels."

"This one isn't too bad for the price."

"Will it make it two more girls?"

"Huh?"

"Will it make it a few hundred miles?"

"Sure. Here's a helmet, gratis. Godspeed."

I handed him the money, took the helmet.

"John," Marnie said, "you can't drive this thing that far."

"The hell I can't."

Because something was cracking through the eggshell of my forgetfulness. I couldn't quite see the wings but the beak was clear, and it was pecking my brain. Some shadowy image and she, She, at the center of it, of course. We were in the trailer. I heard a voice. She said something, She, the ever-present She, the Shiva-She, and She was saying, "What'd I tell you about that? You leave my things alone when I'm not here. I should whoop your ass good."

I was sitting on it now, right in the dealership. I started it up.

"But John, we've hardly had a chance to talk."

"You're innocent, cleared."

"But I want to know what's going on. Didn't you know—calling ahead—like a chain letter—"

Too late, because I roared out of her sentence, as fast as a man can roar on a moped, toward the door I kicked open with one leg, maintaining my balance out of desperation not to fall backwards in time. If I didn't move fast, that bird was gonna crack clear through that shell and swoop down on me.

I hit the road at top speed, forty-five miles an hour, with a laptop strapped to my back. I headed for the two-lane highway, wondering if it was legal. I had the son of Dapple beneath me and the sun of revelation above. I pulled down the helmet mask and watched the world turn green. I was in a fog and not exactly racing along. What I needed was a drink, but I was going to torment myself with this demonic shadow until that drink would seem the holy grail.

I assumed the wind might clean my clothes or at least refresh them with fumes. It wasn't the manliest of two wheels but then no Harley would have been deemed suitable, just as tattoos would have looked ridiculous on me, earrings and adornments of any kind like a housewife trying to wear her daughter's clothes, and the Road Runner's beep-beep of a horn just enough to scare off any frogs, squirrels or rabbits who dared cross my path. Even the helmet seemed unnecessary, for I could only fall in slow motion or splat against a trucker's windshield like a mosquito. The helmet's only use was the tinted mask's graceful drainage of color from this world that exhausted my senses. It could not be said I zoomed nor rumbled but rather sputtered, with all but baseball cards on the spokes.

I was moving straight west now, toward three more towns—unless I found the answer in one before the next. The last was near that place called Mercy, where perhaps I might find some at the end of this journey.

Thinking backwards through these women was a tricky business, the way time sped and slowed between affairs. The first two towns I would hit were much like my home, places in between, nameless with Congressional representatives who didn't even know these voters existed. Number one was only an hour ahead, the next another hour, and then the last less than that.

Suddenly I saw the world the way a hawk might, cool and crisp, with potential nesting spots everywhere in the expanse. In a sense, my journey was speeding up, even as I was slowing down. I was near the end of the puzzle, although I had a feeling the last piece was missing.

Highway Something or Other wasn't the smoothest route. Maybe it was Route 666. To confirm that suspicion, the first and only bar I could find was a hut surrounded by motorcycles. I pulled between a pair of Harleys and removed my helmet. Not exactly Peter Fonda. Two bikers came out of the bar, land-based pirates. I just hoped they weren't related to Chartrise, who lived but twenty minutes away in an A-frame home she called her teepee and from which she distributed astrological advice. My Chartrise with her magic fingers, no quarter required or given. I looked forward to seeing her; I dreaded seeing her. After all, one of these days, she might be right about the future, but it was the past she had almost seen.

Meanwhile, the bikers did not seem too concerned about the past or future. One said, "Rice machine."

"You stupid fuck," came the reply, "it's a moped."

"Then it's a Spic rider. Probably got waders for crossing the river."

"Italian, asshole. Hey, man, why you riding that thing? You're gonna grind your nuts off."

"Got no choice," I said.

"You wanna buy this guy a drink? Let's go back in and buy him a drink."

So I went inside, surrounded by men who had all but Viking horns. Must have been about twenty of them, each drunker than the next, in leather, the crevices of their jackets and pants dusted by the road, their minds possibly dusted by something else. Yet they treated me not as some fool on a moped but a fellow traveler, albeit one not too educated in the fineries of two-wheel machinery. I had more than a few offers to trade in the moped for an old bike. They would probably donate mine as training wheels for their abandoned children.

They bought me one beer after the next, separated by shots of tequila, and a camaraderie formed. I told them about my task at hand and received all manner of advice about weapons, detective-proof burial grounds, phony papers, how to legally change a name and disappear, and what a visit from a biker at three in the morning could accomplish in a lady gone Macbeth, high in the britches, for two hundred dollars.

When I refused these suggestions, they bought me even more drinks and raised their glasses high. And just when I was feeling safe, when I began to understand these men would die for one another, for no reason but to prove that they would die for one another, the bartender slapped a measuring tape on the counter and announced, "Time for the yardstick game." And then they all unzipped their leather trousers.

Finale

"Where you going?" somebody shouted. "It's just a damn game."

But remembering locker room surveys, I had no desire for the booby prize. I ran to the parking lot and kickstarted the moped. In my rearview mirror, I saw them amble out as if they had rockets and I a go-kart. One minute later, five of them surrounded me.

"We'll escort you."

"But I can barely—" I started to say when I lost all balance and tipped over, a most undramatic crash that left me at the side of the road as my escorts laughed, waved goodbye and wished me luck. The only casualty was the laptop, which when I turned it on displayed the green light of my isolation and the red light of my mind—my mind and only my mind.

Unbelievably, the moped started right up again. I headed for the House of Chartrise. I didn't believe in any of that fortune-telling shit, but I was starting to think it believed in me. Anyway, I would ask a fortune teller this: "Tell me something that already happened. That ought to be easy." She was almost ready to pass that test. And so, perhaps best not to administer it. Anyway, I knew that when I saw her, our student-teacher relationship would reverse. She would seduce me, and she would administer the test. The exam I had procrastinated away my whole life was not multiple choice, nor true/false. I was about to learn the correct response was always true *and* false.

I drove with eyes half-closed, and I was dreaming even though I remained conscious. For half a minute, I was Magritte, bowler hats sailing past my head.

Earthquake 5.0

Surrounded by my own asshole, I am.

But I still amble with shopworn senses

and cannot be disguised, nor camouflaged:

Every town rats out the feminine.

Donkey highways, good spots for hell peeking.

Cleared by hips, conceived in Vietnam.

Banana-ripe in Bakersfield—blew it.

You grow, you pay. A world of seeds and wind.

They'll true-fix me three million miles from here.

Just the bird-fish and me, swimming, flying.

Pygmies float past, innocent of diamonds.

We've left those behind; no merchants here.

Three

True: I lacked borders. I was not a proper nation. I was a reservation, implying something more was owed me. Something had been reserved that would not be given. The world certainly had its reservations about me, and I had mine about it. We were in two camps, and one day soon, somebody would yell, "Charge!"

But for now, I had to hang those bowler hats on their hooks. I climbed off the moped in Chartrise's driveway, the world hazed by a sheer curtain of sun, birds humming.

The House of Chartrise was a modern pyramid, ode to superstitious ages past, within its walls a woman who, though she might have been the devil if the fundamentalists were correct, would ease the path to hell with a carpet of roses and a spell that made the toes twinkle. She could have put Adolph Hitler out of his and our misery with a foot massage. I worried what she would tell me, for her predictions had a way of coming true. As mentioned, I do not believe in superpowers, ESP, PSI, or even synchronicity. What I believed was that she planted seeds in well-tilled brains. The seeds sprouted, and one couldn't help but climb their stalks, those stalks leading to the destinations she predicted, set in motion by her very green thumb.

She answered the door in astral-pajamas, stars and planets shimmering on the silk. She touched my shoulder. She always knew how to touch me. "I knew you were coming. A bird told me, like in the Bible. Let me see your palm." She took my hand, dropped it. "Too much dirt. It was a blackbird, now that I think of it. It had a message for you: Don't continue this journey."

"What do the rabbits have to say?"

"Sarcasm: another sign of fear. But I can barely hear the lies; your truth is louder. Come inside."

It was as if no time had passed since we met those many years ago, when on the recommendation of a gas station attendant I had stopped for a "reading," just for kicks, and found myself falling in love. It wasn't mystery, opposites attract or any of that. When she touched me, her hands clasped a boy and said, "Shh, it's okay." The boy listened. The boy felt comforted. But sooner or later, the boy would grow old enough to suspect that it wasn't okay at all. Even then, he hoped magical mother would transform him.

I remembered how she had touched something I did not want touched, a memory that resisted probing. Anyway, after a while, all that crystal ball shit got on my nerves. I left with the hangover of several hallucinogenic experiences and the sense that I had been interrogated while under the influence.

Still, that first week stayed with me. I longed to repeat it, to curl inside a loop and let those days wrap their arms around me, for all time, forever. It could not be. Anyone who understood what I wanted had to understand why I wanted it, and I didn't want to understand that myself. As soon as they approached my secret place, hide and seek was over. They couldn't find me. I ran too fast.

"Go outside and wait for me," she said. "I'll be there in a moment."

I found a lawnchair and from it surveyed the backyard, an open territory blurry with dense trees, a place that welcomed me, where one might see any number of animals bound across the landscape as if Jesus himself might leap into creation and grant one wish to everyone.

"Let us stop preying upon one another, Lord," the animals would say.

"Let me know all," Chartrise would say.

Finale

"Cure me of these skin and bones," I would beg, "and let me become air."

In this plushness, I felt my wish had been granted, for I could breathe without thinking or needing or wanting. I had no wish for wisdom. The less I knew, the better.

She emerged from the house with a pitcher of tea. I knew it was no refreshment but some kind of liquid drug, probably mushrooms or maybe LSD. I was still drunk, but that was fading fast, the intense concentration required to reach this place alive on a scooter having worn away intoxication. She sat in the chair beside mine and poured two glasses, handing me one.

"Peyote? Psilocybin?"

"So distrusting," she said. "Just drink it."

She would never harm me. Not on purpose. Only revelations could harm me. As above, so below.

I drank. At first, nothing happened. But in times past, it could take an hour before the world started doubling and tripling while the props that held the sky aloft collapsed, time went gooey, and spoken words became a scribble of calligraphy. With all those mushroom trips between us, our bond was molecular. Transmutation seemed possible. We could bend metal, move through walls, swap bodies, anything. In the best moments, I thought she might just be able to tender me a man acceptable by all the world's standards.

It seemed prudent to address reality while one still existed. "Are you trying to kill me?"

"Me? I don't kill spiders or flies."

"You're not having a joke at my expense, with letters of threat and emails of malice? If so, welcome to the friar's club. My roast never ends."

"John," she said, touching my hand, "you think I'd do that?"

"No, I don't, but I'm running out of suspects. Now I'm turning into one. Seems a little fish wants to catch a bigger fish—me—by tying a noose around her neck and then letting the noose grab mine when they cut her loose."

"You're eating too much red herring."

"I'm not eating much of anything. And I've got a feeling I'll have even less of an appetite in about three minutes."

"You use that number a lot, you know? Three: the magic number of jokes but also the completion of a process."

She took my wrist and worked a chakra or power spot or who knows what until my blood became a river of Valium, saturating my system.

"Let go. You know that you can."

"The world is at war with me, my nation divided. I've got a gospel-singing demon for a wife and a past that tracks me down. I feel like Ahab, only I swapped places with the whale and now I've got a spear up my ass. I'm out of money. My wife controls the bank. I hear obscene spirituals in my sleep. I've slept with orange women. A gang of bikers just tried to measure my manhood. Even revelatory bumperstickers can't save me."

"Miles to go before you sleep."

"Please."

"Not much further, though. I can help. I'm rich. I've got a stable of fortune tellers who operate phones all over the state."

"Like a fortune-telling pimp, you mean?"

"We tell people what they know but can't admit they know."

"And what if they're better off not knowing?"

"Then we keep quiet. You don't really think a little dust would keep me from reading your palm?"

She was haloed, glowing with witchy goodness. Whatever she'd put in those drinks was kicking up another kind of dust.

"There's a bug on the arm of your chair, watching you. Is it 'praying' or 'preying' mantis?"

I smashed it with my palm. "Neither."

"That wasn't very nice."

Finale

We sat silently for another ten minutes or possibly six hours. Moths swooped in air-show formations. Six-foot-long dragonflies soared. A bat flew overhead and landed on a tree, struck a Bela Lugosi pose. New constellations formed. They all looked like genitals.

"You see that?"

"I'm getting naked," she said.

Off came the pajamas. On the lawn, she twirled, Shirley Temple on mushrooms, which by now I knew was exactly what I had consumed because my stomach cramped as it always did whenever I ate truffles. I laughed and laughed, but that only encouraged her. She was Ginger Rogers, Barishnikov, Nijinksi. She flipped genders like a blackjack/jane dealer.

"You can do better?" she said.

"I'm a ballerina, Sabrina."

I took off my clothes and went Fred Astaire straight across the sky. We kept at it for another half hour, or three, and then we collapsed on the grass. Astronomy above and—with my luck—hell below. Was the plane on which we danced purgatory? If the Christian way must be true, and Lord how I hoped it was not, I could accept purgatory as my destination, for it must be quiet, so very quiet. I didn't think I could stand a heaven with eternal family picnics and choruses singing, "Lord, Lord, Lord, how we praise you, let us praise you, hallelujah, alleluia, and whatever else rhymes with ya." After 6.9 million years, or a week, all that bliss would get a little tired, even angel flight monotonous. "Can somebody kindly shove that horn up Gabriel's ass? He ain't no Miles Davis."

Nor did I want to sodomize goats or rub cat's blood from head to toe or bump ass with witches or suck Satan's tit. I had made no bargains, or if I had, I must have sold my soul on the cheap.

No, purgatory would suit me fine, just fence-sitting and mugwumping. Quite peaceful on a fence, and nobody shoots until you jump one way or the other. "Ha ha, I'm on both your properties, so whatchoo gonna do?"

Chartrise said, "What on earth are you thinking about?"

"This."

We fucked like teenagers. It was all so chemical. The coyotes sang Edith Piaf, the fireflies ganged up and made a spotlight, and the ants tickled our funny bones.

Then we slept under a sky that sagged and leaked, a fat water balloon of galaxies, which might have induced panic but instead calmed me. I'd knew I'd keep running rampant through these crumbs of sand and dirt, skittering and scattering, driven by some internal mechanism sidetracked and fucked up by thought. But the wrench in the works had been temporarily disabled. I was now a Natural Man, yes, no longer made supernatural by this brain that formulated riddles without solutions. I had terminated that demented game show host who held blue cards with questions on one side but no answers on the other. But he would be rehired.

What was the ape's biggest mistake? The upward slanted statement, pointed at the sky, sloping for solution. And what was the first question, rephrased in our vernacular? "Why you hit me in the head with that bone, motherfucker? I was just sitting here minding my business, you stupid fuck. How'd you like that bone up your ass?" The start of all our troubles. But if we could stay at the center of our doubt, in our true position, marked by cartography, plotted in longitude and latitude at the precise location of the great confusion, would we not finally escape our dilemma by refusing to attempt an escape? Like the Chinese fingercuff?

But then the balloon explodes, all those stars sucking into my nose, choking me. Now I felt murderous. My head reeled in memories. I was a fisherman holding a string of spit-coating catfish. They smelled like sex.

I went inside and found the liquor cabinet. I drank scotch until I vomited those fish on the floor, and then I stumbled and fell into an imaginary mess, for I had not vomited—not physically.

Finale

"And if you got anything else to say," I told that distant self who wanted to know what he could not and should not know, "I'll shove a clavicle through your fucking heart."

Someone helped me up, Chartrise, of course. I don't know if it's possible, but I swear she radiated love, and I needed a very special form of chemotherapy.

I awoke on the couch at two o'clock the next afternoon.

"I dragged you there," Chartrise said from the other couch. "I'm sorry I didn't find you until dawn."

She was sitting in a wicker chair, bruised, slouched in weird angles. She was smoking, something she only did when she felt the paranormal had betrayed her, when what she called fate boxed her ears and whispered into the ringing, "This is all bullshit and you know it, this shaman routine of yours." Because during the brief period when I lived with her, she experienced those doubts one night, and out came the cigarettes. She ignited the sick feeling within and blew it out the chimney. She exhaled the realization that her times were not the Middle Ages, that only imbeciles bought the modern Merlin's act. She admitted as much that night in bed, insisting I assure her that she was no phony. So I said, "You're no phony, Chartrise. You're the real thing." Like Coca-Cola, I wanted to add, with fizz and a kick, but junk just the same, caffeine not magic, just chemistry, like you and me.

But now I saw she had a letter in hand. She was the one? Out of all these women, the least likely, the one I considered pure of heart—discounting her occupation—had been the woman who threatened my life? And then tried to wrap me in a murder rap?

"Why'd you have to bother me? Why'd you have to send me on this idiot's journey?"

"What," she said, "in the hell are you talking about?"

"That's one of your threatening letters, no?"

She tossed it on the floor. It landed three feet from me. It took me as many minutes to crawl there. And then I saw the envelope had an official government seal, from the U.S. Army itself, postmarked years before, and unopened.

"Where was I to forward it?" she said. "Who knew where you went? You filed your taxes here, remember, at the last moment, April 14th? So they must have used this address."

Well, I remembered the night before just fine, hallucination that it was, and everything I had learned told me to shred the letter and leave whatever answer lay within as shrouded as it had always been. But then that goddamn human being within me made its demand. I opened the letter and read.

"Well?"

"They used to burn those villages. That's where they found them, her village, in a tunnel underneath a hut. ID'd by teeth. Goddamn teeth. The Vietnamese dug them up years later. Nothing here about a burial, no words of remorse, no blah blah blah at all. They were NVA, Chartrise. And they were incinerated."

She stubbed her cigarette. Like Superman, she heard a sudden call for her powers. To the phone booth!

"Let me run you a bath."

"Yes."

"A bath with candles."

I hadn't realized until then that I remained naked. She helped me to the tub. It took all my concentration to step inside without breaking my neck. She started the water, and the years ran through the faucet, filling the tub, surrounding me. I soaked in the mud of a mad world. I floated in paddy water. The candles were Sun, the smoke my father, the fragrance incense for the dead. They had left me alone, and I was still alone.

Chartrise sat on the toilet, watching. How could someone help and hurt me at the same time? Ah, she was a physician of sorts.

Finale

"Whatever you do," I said, "don't tell me the future."

I fell asleep with her watching over me. As I've said, I don't give a shit about dreams. Damn their premonitions, their loose associations, their jabberwocky hints. But this dream was different, for Sun took Chartrise's place on the toilet. She leaned toward me, touched my cheeks, kissed my forehead.

"Be cool, my napalm baby," she said.

"It's time to go," my invisible father said. "Nothing left to betray."

I felt a strange sense of forgiveness. I was born to war memories, a history as senseless as my autobiography, but Christ how I demarcated this life with signposts blown helter-skelter. No wonder I was lost. No wonder I never stayed in one place. Los Angeles was Vietnam, Saigon was Saginaw, Michigan, and in between the potholes over which I drove were really blackholes that sent me to these places, back and forth, at light speed.

I awoke, thinking how wonderful that I hadn't experienced another shaker. Then the next one started.

Earthquake 6.0

Goodbye Father, goodbye Sun. So long, ghosts.
I shirk your spirits, Vietnam blackholes.
But this land troubles me. We watch Hitler
from the couch. He's on TV. Now we see.
I must exhale these associations.
My heart? History poured junk inside it,
grown from poppies, dropped from B-52s.
Christ would roast us in the apocalypse?
The Christian story poisoned the garden.
All creation shadowed, even the Sun.
So I say: WE do the forgiving here.
Sick of red herring, I say no blessing.
With calmness, oooooooh, I am close. I mean, om.
Running to the quake. Can't you hear its call?

Two

Was I running to my destruction? No, I was running to my reconstruction, or so I thought. But the civil war had not yet ended.

I left "town" while Chartrise was sleeping. It was too hard to say good-bye, for she seemed the embodiment of my secret belief that there could be some metallurgic transformation of myself into a stronger, better man. And if I listened to her about the number three, well, then, she might have been the one. But that force within me, forged by evolution, I suppose, demanded, in blood treaty, that I continue to the end...or was it the beginning? I was a kid who'd learned the oven was hot but couldn't help but touch it one more time. Actually, two more times, in this case, because I had two women to go and then it was back to Rosie, if Rosie remained at home. If not, I would become a monkey monk, hairy old Bodhisattva with "ooo-ooo-aghh-aghh" for a mantra and a banana for a walking stick. Jane Goodall would stop by for visits and I would tell her what I had learned—or rather, unlearned—by pressing buttons for fruit-cup rewards.

It was both easy and impossible to remain a good humor man riding that moped to Caitlin's house, Caitlin meaning, she had told me, virginal beauty. If Caitlin asked which woman I loved the best or most, I could hardly tear off my shirt and display Rosie on my chest. If, that is, Caitlin wasn't in the convent, where she had sworn she would go after I left her, claiming that sleeping with me had caused lesbian desires and the concern that she might soon place ads in auto swappers for "clean and sophisticated professional women, bi-curious." And so I was going from the House of Chartrise to the House of Our Lord. Only an hour divided them.

All these women were marchers in the pilgrimage. They thought turtle eggs or bumperstickers or Big Boy keys or magic dust would bring salvation. But I thought we already lived in the land of the pilgrim's pride? Did not God shed his grace on thee? Was not God to mend our every flaw and confirm our souls in self-control? Were not paths to be wrought through wilds of thought? But when would the rocks break their silence and let us know the deal was done? The whole goddamned country was mixed up, village idiots jumping hurdles, and it was as easy to forgive the one-thousand mystics and Alabama snake charmers longing for the apocalypse as it was to pin a blue ribbon to a handicapped kid who'd sprinted underneath a hurdle and won the Special Olympics.

Vietnam, for napalm skies, for napalm's sake, for heaven's sake...How far I had traveled from my birthplace nation. Another half-breed thinking earthbound linkup with the other sex would somehow pipe me into some known, remembered juncture.

And now I stood two steps from proving something else: Maybe I really had written the letter myself. With the tricks my memory played, it was possible. I might have lost myself in that Chartrise induced-flashback. In our very first week together, Chartrise had scrambled my brains so many times there remained no yolk, only egg whites.

As I bumped to a stop in Caitlin's driveway, I breathed the lonely agnostic sigh. Catholics were kinfolk to me, psychic fuck-ups, shadowed by endless mysteries, fueled by guilt but the gas line hidden. Mine also remained hidden. I could not confess its source to a priest. I wasn't even sure it was my fault. But something about me had been botched from the beginning. I less wanted to be forgiven for it than to find out what it was, because by now I knew that truth is a gap, a crack fillable with anything, but never to the brim. I filled that fissure, but the gap kept growing wider, the way it did for everybody, until it would swallow us, then spits us out with new religions and hairdos.

So there I was again, standing before the great and bottomless hole.

She waited for me on the porch, wearing a sky-blue sweatsuit like Mother Mary at the exercise club. I suppose even the Virgin Mother had to watch the thighs. Caitlin stood with her head to one side and a queer expression—not that kind of queer but the 18th century version, as though she might swoon—I suddenly understood why they all seemed to know I was coming. I remembered the shards of Marnie's last sentence to me: "Didn't you know—calling ahead—like a chain letter—"

Because years before I had blabbed like a schoolgirl the details of each past affair to every women who followed, and they must have passed a note back in time after I confronted each with my accusation: "He's coming. The imbecile thinks one of us is trying to kill him. Now he thinks we'll get him on a murder rap, too. He'll believe anything. He'll show up in however many hours it takes him to get there. Lock your doors. Duct tape your bra straps."

Caitlin tapped her foot, *tap, tap, tap,* still the most impatient quasi-virgin who ever lived. Quasi because the moment I'd found my way inside her, I'd been shown the way out. Then she pushed me off and underwent her conversion, right before my eyes. She flipped and flopped and said something about mommy and daddy and for a second I expected her to show me a school bus ID proving she was fourteen years old, not twenty-one, as she'd told me. Then she made me go downstairs, and then she made me leave. She had explained she always suspected she might not like men quite enough, and that before our speedy sex, lasting as long as the space shuttle took to cross the Mississippi, she had imagined for a moment that I was a woman. And that striking image had, actually, struck her, I believe. For her last words to me were, "I'm joining the convent."

I had to admit, I felt a little proud at that moment. I had made a nun. Presto. I figured that if my luck failed and the great god of judgement really did exist, then I had earned a bonus point, a mitigating factor my heaven-appointed public defender would employ in my defense, to get me into purgatory, parole for the semi-damned.

Tap, tap, tap went the foot. Before I even climbed off the moped, she shouted, "I didn't send a letter. Now go away."

I approached, and she retreated. I was a black guy in an elevator filled with old white women. Still, I kept moving. I wanted to know where she was looking now, for what treasure pot of redemption she was digging in her holy track suit.

"What, you're gonna hurt me? I told you, it wasn't me. It wasn't any of us. Why don't you leave us alone?"

"Mary, I just want to talk."

"Caitlin."

"Sorry—the color of your—I just want to talk, Caitlin."

"Yeah? Come inside then, for five minutes. I'm looking at my watch right now. You're down to four minutes and fifty seconds. Forty, thirty-nine—"

"Thirty-nine steps to nothing?"

So we went inside. She stood in the corner. I remained at the screen door, like a fly. I surveyed the room, everywhere religious candles, angels on walls; interior decorating by a gay priest.

"You're a nun?"

"No. I left the convent."

"Temptation?"

"Leave me alone. But God bless you on the way out."

"God bless me? How 'bout gazoontite?"

"Atheist."

"Agnostic. Even that doesn't capture the gist of—"

"Same difference. Now would you go?"

"Can I sit down? Just for a minute?"

"I suppose you'll try to seduce me now? Don't make me laugh."

"Just for a minute."

"Go ahead and talk. But I'm staying here."

It seemed all my ex-girlfriends had created their own religions. It was a step in the right direction, but for them, too, miles to go. Maybe that was the problem with the country: too many miles. No garment could stay tightly knit over such distances. Every comforter frayed and exposed one to the cold plains. Same thing in the city, gusts down the avenues. That's why alcohol was big: a fireplace of sorts, the heat temporary, an illusion...but always, anything better than nothing.

"Yesterday," I said, "I learned my parents died in Vietnam."

"Sorry to hear that. I hope they rest in peace. I'll say a prayer for them— or would that insult you?"

"They don't respond to prayer, I'm quite sure. Communists, you see, working the other side. Another religion, of course, but at least they tried."

"You must have wondered all these years what happened to them?"

"I knew they were blowing around. It was only a matter of where their ashes landed."

"Boy, you're cold. Is there nothing in this world you love?"

"I love plenty, but something always gets in the way. I don't get to keep it. I'm a pawn shop, everything just passing through. Or a museum, beauty blocked by tourists with their fat—"

"About that night. I still consider myself a virgin."

"So that's what you tell yourself."

"It didn't count."

"Your God doesn't seem a detail man."

"Aren't you getting tired of this—persona? You're not the man you think you are. You didn't even deflower me. The flower never broke."

"The petals bent."

"Whatever. And where to next?"

"You already know, don't you? Holly's house."

"Holly. The last one, huh?"

"Well, the letter came from California, and my first two girlfriends, they won't ever leave Michigan; they can't get over the lakes. Stuck in the mitten. It's a catcher's mitt, that state. So, yes, Holly's the last one."

"Well, she knows you're coming. In fact, I received an email from her, if you'd like to read it."

This time a paper was handed to me.

> When John comes to see you, please pass on my invitation. I'm waiting, along with a surprise. A surprise party, in fact, to which you're all invited. Won't it be fun, all us girls together? And then we'll tell him the truth. And you can tell him I said so.

"What truth?"

"You'll have to wait and see."

"You're all going to kill me at once, then pin it on me?"

"Not exactly."

I thought about this for a moment. What man has a chance to meet his ex-lovers in one house, like some kind of X-rated Victorian novel, in the countryside where Holly's dead husband's second home must still exist? It wasn't far from San Francisco, not exactly wine country but close. And there, the denouement would occur. For there must be one, if this plot was to unfold, if this origami of a journey was to ever reveal its pre-dotted lines. Might not Hercule Poirot emerge—into a drawing room, of course—tug his mustache and say, "Ladies and gentlemen, what we have here is a mystery, only it is not really a mystery. More of a riddle. No, it's not even a riddle but a child's prank, for all criminals are children. Anyway, one of you is guilty. One of you stuck your hand in the jar, and though you scrubbed chocolate from your hands, I know who you are. And now, I shall reveal you."

"Fine," I said, "I accept the invitation. Only, I'm not riding on a goddamn moped for another two hours. You're driving."

"Okay, I'll drive. But you're sitting in the back seat."

"You're safe with me. I'm no lesbian."

"Sure about that?"

On the way out, a boy tossed a newspaper at us. I caught it and took it with me to the car. As we pulled out of the driveway, I read all about it: nuclear proliferation; flying rocks and helicopters on the Israeli border; terrorists in the suburbs, bankrupted dioceses; a 56-year-old woman who gave birth to ten children; DNA with strings attached to everything; the stealing of a local man's power saw; horoscopes; scandal in the wide world of sports; tornadoes in the Midwest; strife in the Philippines; upheaval in world markets; a shortage of oysters; this month's phases of the moon; obituaries and birth notices of people I would never know; marriage licences and divorce filings for couples I would never meet; bowling scores; advertisements for everything; classifieds selling everything back; lost and found dogs and cats; the destruction of the environment.

I imagined another headline: "WANDERER FAKES LOCAL WOMAN'S SUICIDE: WANTED FOR MURDER IN THE FIRST DEGREE."

I scrunched the newspaper into a gray ball and tossed it out the window. It whipsawed down the highway, shredding in a truck's gust, the narrative splitting apart. The strewn words, separated, recombined, then separated again, once and for all. The divorce had been finalized, but the arguments remained.

Christ, I was tired all the time, a dream ready every second of the day, like tears of the broken-hearted. I might have cried, but instead those dreams began to seep. They didn't care if I fell asleep. They would get to me one way or the other.

Earthquake 7.0

What can all-American children do
at play in the fields of the Lord's novel?
Me, still in the egg, and I can't crack it.
This door closed. Don't knock, pal, and don't you peck.
Anyway, this world's made of eggshell, too.
Crack one, you've got another one to crack,
like Russian nesting dolls. Eggs bear more eggs.
Our verdict? Guilty, for biology?
Dark nights in Africa, at the ocean's curve,
unable to perceive the earth 'tis round,
we built civilizations on fiction.
We war at story hour, our aim "The End."

One

Eggs, eggs, eggs: All these dreams boiled down to eggs.

Appropriately enough, a semi-virgin drove as I sat in back watching the road the way one always watches it toward the end of a journey: "What happened to all those promises you made, road? Broke every damn one of them, and I fell for it again." But when I looked at the map and focused on our location, I felt that one promise remained, that of solution, resolution.

"I'm happy," Caitlin said.

"Really? You never get the—urge?"

"I'm filled with urges. But once you get the trick of denying urges, denial is more fun than surrender."

"Or you just tell yourself that?"

"Shut up."

I was thinking of finally calling Rosie, to let her know I was almost home. Still, I wanted to punish her for all those blows I had absorbed. That was my back slap and slap back. I bet she thought I wouldn't make it twenty miles without her. Then she upped the bet to fifty, and by now she must have thought I was never coming home. And maybe I wasn't. It all depended.

"This house is in the middle of nowhere," Caitlin said.

"It's where we fucked, to exorcize the memory of her husband."

"Like you're shocking me, John Thomas."

"Jonathan."

"You don't like your short little name, your innie-weenie real name?"

"So call me Johnny. We're traveling companions."

"No, I'm your friend. We *all* are. Otherwise, why travel all these miles for your sake?"

"Group assassination?"

"I wonder what you see through those eyes of yours."

"Coyotes singing Edith Piaf."

"You must mystify the maker."

"I sure the fuck hope so because there's never been a man as mystified as me."

"It's your parents' fault."

"And who's the fault of them?"

"Their parents. That's how evil works."

"Evil. You happen to catch any priests pitching communal wafers in the aisles, playing fetch with the alter boys? But sin is a forgivable mystery when it comes to that. Isn't that what the Pope says?"

"I don't need the Pope."

"Well, you've got one, on a rope."

"I make up my own rules, according to my interpretation."

"That's what Protestants do, not Catholics."

We picked up speed after that. And then she said, "You know what? You just love to confuse people. You think you outwit everybody, but you're outwitting yourself."

"I can't outwit myself. If I'm trying to confuse you, it's just to get us on equal footing."

"More like a slippery slope."

"To hell, right?"

"Not for me to say. So tell me more about this Holly. You never did say much about her when we met, except in passing."

"It happened in passing, in more ways than one. She was Chapter One, you might say, from my Book of Wanderings. She was just widowed, hanging out in some bar. We got talking. She zeroed in on me. I knew what I was, a trick of memory, to help her forget a dead husband. It was a fair lie: I was trying to forget my mother. So we ended up back at her house. Together, we did plenty of forgetting. She always wore fishnet stockings, and she always said, "Hmm," like she was just about to finish a crossword puzzle she'd been working on for thirty years. I think the answers contained her lovers' names. It didn't take long before she said, 'Well...' and then I knew it was time for me to go. She was just a kid, really, like you, only she had experience. Maybe a little brighter."

"Thanks."

"Yeah, but she was no kid, if you counted her rings. I wonder what happened to her? I always wonder what happened to all of you, but then I remember you probably never wondered about me."

"I suppose you want me to say I wondered?"

"Hmm."

We took a tunnel-like road, arced by trees, light dimmed by a stained-glass ceiling of forestry.

"I'll tell you something else," I said. "This party wasn't Holly's idea. Oh, maybe she decided to host because she ended up with that house somehow. But I bet it was someone else."

"Like who? Me?"

"No, not you, Sister Caitlin. Somebody dastardly, like Azal. She's probably trying to deconstruct me. I'm the guy in that game Operation. She sets off the buzzers off with a pair of tweezers...on purpose."

For a moment, I thought I was right, but panic changed my mind, for we had made it through that tunnel and were soon in the driveway of Holly's house.

As we parked, Caitlin probably couldn't wait for the denouement. I plotted my escape. If necessary, I would beat it out the door and hit the main road with both thumbs in the air. If a psychotic stopped to pick me up, we'd have plenty to share before he slit my throat and dumped me on the side of the road in a garbage bag.

"Here we are," Caitlin said. "Looks like a church, don't it?"

"Just what I need. Drop me off and I'll confess. Pick me up in four years."

We got out of the car. I stopped for a moment. Holly had been my first real love or would have been had there been more time. She had a body made for men like me, those who long to be cupped and babied, only she wasn't meant to baby and lacked the children to prove it. She belonged in the Jonathan Thomas Museum of Modern Women, but who wants to be museumed and forbidden from touch? Not Holly. Holly was strictly hands on and completely interactive.

Caitlin yanked me toward the door. She rang the bell. Holly answered, still wearing fishnet stockings, the rest of her in black, too. Behind her stood Mary, Azal, Kerrie, Aquamarine, Chartrise. They all wore black and some wore veils. I was waiting for Johnny Cash to rise from the dead and play *Ring of Fire*.

"Oh," Caitlin said, "I didn't think to wear black."

"It doesn't matter," Holly said. "Come in, John."

"Come in, John," they all repeated.

"Have a seat," said Holly.

I sat on the couch. They roamed and stalked, sipping coffee. Some held Bibles. I thought it might be one of those interventions, but I was sober as Bill W. The only one who looked the least uncomfortable, as if she were having doubts about the whole affair, was Kerrie. She winked at me and smiled, as if to say, "Don't take this seriously, John."

The others milled about. It seemed part of their plan that I have a moment alone with Holly.

"Well," she said, "how are you?"

Finale

"Not bad, considering."

"Considering what?"

"That you're trying to kill me."

"Hmm."

"Oh, right: 'Hmm.' If you remember, that's what you said the first night: 'Hmm.' As if that answered my question."

"Actually, it did."

"It wasn't much of an answer."

"Is that what you want, answers? Okay. You're a little weird, sexually."

"Meaning what?"

"I don't know, exactly. That's why I said, 'Hmm.'"

"Then why am I here?"

"You were coming, anyway, weren't you?"

"And how did you know that?"

"Look," Azal said, "here it comes now."

And it came. It came rolling out on wheels. It was just the right length, about six feet long with plenty of leg room. Somebody had given it a shove from its hiding place.

"Welcome to your funeral," Azal said. "Here's your coffin. No need to climb inside: You're already dead."

The first words that came to mind were, "What the fuck?" but I couldn't speak. I always wondered who would attend my funeral, whether I would watch from above and count the friends left at the end. But these were no friends.

"You *are* dead, Jonathan Thomas," Chartrise said. "There's no need to fear, for we're all reborn many times in this life."

"Amen," Caitlin said.

"Even those who don't deserve it," Mary said.

"Even those who run from everyone they love," Aquamarine said.

"Even dictators," Azal said.

"If it weren't for you already being dead," Holly said, "we might have made love one last time. Hmm."

"You didn't miss much," Mary said.

Then they talked amongst themselves, as if I weren't present. I wasn't altogether sure I *was* there. Possible, I really was dead. Had any of this happened? Had I really traveled all this way, seen all these women, one by one? Had I covered every mile? Had I found my way into more paranoid subplots than Joe McCarthy? Or had I made them up? Was I dead before any of this happened? Was I gone long before any marriage to Rosie? Was this a hell designed for wanderers? And where was Johnny Cash? Because I fell into that ring, and the flames were rising higher.

"He wasn't so bad."

"He was funny, sometimes."

"Just had to look past his many shortcomings, ha ha."

"Remember the way he laughed?"

"He did laugh a lot. He found strange things funny."

"He sure did. He considered things funny that would make anyone else cry."

"He was special. Oh, but not special like that, ha ha."

"Not the best lay I ever had."

"Size does matter."

"I wouldn't know. I've never really—"

"Oh, you knew. You just didn't know you knew."

"Johnny Cash," I said. "Johnny, help me."

"You hear something?"

"I think I hear a ghost."

"Shhh: He might be present here amongst us."

"Be respectful girls."

"Why's he talking about Johnny Cash? He means Dion. That's who sang *his* song."

Finale

"Now he thinks he's Johnny Cash. He's no Johnny Cash."

"*We're* the ones wearing black."

I still had legs—at least it seemed I did—and I ran.

Kerrie grabbed my arm. "I didn't want to come, but they talked me into it. Don't you see we're just trying to scare you into someone new and better? Scare you out of this world you've built?"

"I've got no bumperstickers," I shouted, if I still had a mouth, and then I bolted out the door toward the main route. "You're all trying to kill me. You're all in on it."

They chased me, be they ghosts or lovers or both, but I was running faster, sped by supernatural legs or maybe just the sight of the coffin that held, as they claimed, some old me within it.

I saw an eighteen-wheeler headed from a mile down the road. It looked a hell of a lot like the one in the parking lot of the Giant Travel Plaza. I was sure I even recognized the driver's baseball hat. I ran and ran and crossed the traffic. I waved my arms like flags. And then I ate seventy-thousand pounds of steel and glass.

Earthquake 8.0: The Big One

Listen. Shhh, shhh. Endure a moment more.

Take in Lord Halogen's Sun. Puff a pipe,

sing an ode. It will all be revealed soon.

You'll see your red and white angels descend.

For now, let the ripe grapes do the singing.

Stomp a fresh glass. There's time, plenty of time.

Just call me Johnny Bodhisattva.

This ain't suicide. Quite the opposite.

Uh-oh, here comes the plot. Turn on TV.

Pages of the Koran, Bible, flutter.

Miracle? No. This direction. Hurry...

Zero

I was a new kind of wanderer, one on wheels, whose road was a hospital room. Ex-lovers came to visit, but I told the nurse, "No, not unless one of them is named Janie or Flo."

"Huh?"

"My song."

"What song?"

I was parked in that bed for weeks, and then rehabilitation started. My arms strengthened. I had two fists of iron but I wasn't going anywhere. The rest of me weakened, my legs half-present, amputated at the knees. Couldn't feel my thighs. Needless to say, I would never reproduce, nor could I even put forth the effort. Was it their revenge on me or mine on them? Meanwhile, my mother kept calling, but I hung up every time.

I longed to go home. I wanted to see Rosie, convincing myself this crisis would bring us together, bind us in peace. But Rosie never came to visit. She could no longer fit into a car, much less a plane.

They finally released me in the winter. A special van took me to an airport. I was loaded in like cargo. One hour later, I was unloaded and shipped home in another special van.

Rosie didn't look so happy to see me.

"Dear John," she said. I couldn't figure it out because it sounded like, "Dear John, what have I done?"

"*All* those women were trying to kill me, not just one."

She watched me, shaking her head. "Why wouldn't you take your mother's calls at the hospital? And why won't you answer me now? Why won't you answer anybody?"

"Why should I call her? She got anything to say besides mu-ma blah-blah-blah and maybe something about killing Chinks, Jews and Arabs?"

"Here, take the phone. *You* call her. Just talk to her. Please, John."

What was there to lose, besides my arms, chest and head? I didn't have so far to go before I slept, but then again, it would take me longer to get there. Please, I hoped, not too much longer.

"What do you want?" I said to my would-be mother.

"Well, it's—"

That fucking voice, that anti-mother bellow from the phony womb, with her aprons around my neck and a rolling pin above my head.

She said, "It's—it's almost kind of funny."

"Well, I think I'll hang up now.

"No, John, you don't know the whole story. I sent that letter. I had a friend mail it from San Diego. Only me and Rosie knew, to start. We knew you were about to wander off again."

I should have been surprised. I should have had a heart attack. But sometimes you know what's coming before you know that you know. "I won't be doing any wandering now, will I?"

"But you don't know why you've been wandering. Only I know. Okay, and Rosie knows, too, because I told her so, the only person I ever told. And then I guess Rosie got hold of one of your old girlfriends and spread the word—I mean, the word spread." She sighed. How to say what she was going to say? Because it was going to be something I didn't want to hear. "You don't remember, do you? I had to beat you something awful to keep you from wearing my clothes. I'd come home—but how were you supposed to know any better? That's why they dropped you off, your daddy and his whore. They didn't know what to do when they saw, either. Must have damn near blown their brains out when the doctors dropped that bomb on 'em. Then they dropped it on me. Dropped you, I mean."

"What the hell are you talking about? I was just a baby."

"Just a baby, except they couldn't figure out whether you was a boy or girl. So it ain't no surprise you've been all over the map. Folds of skin all mixed up. How was I supposed to know? It ain't in Dr. Spock."

"What about the birth certificate? They checked off the 'male' box."

"Had to check something. They called it ambivalent genitalia."

"What the fuck is ambivalent genitalia?"

"Ambiguous," Rosie said. "She means ambiguous."

"They thought maybe it was the napalm that caused the birth defect. You could've gone either way, see, boy, girl, or no way at all. Well, that's the way your father and that gook left you: no way at all."

I watched Rosie, but she wouldn't look at me. It was all coming back now: sneaking into Mother's room and slipping on her panty hose until they rode up to my neck. I sure the hell remembered my mother stripping those hose off me, whipping me blind, clocking me so often it was no wonder I never protested when Rosie bitch-slapped me. And now the sex made sense, too, the way I knew what women wanted. *Of course* I knew what they wanted; I was practically one of them, a swipe of the knife from wearing panties instead of jockeys, and looking to climb inside their bodies for good, where maybe I'd feel more at peace than I did in my own testosterone-challenged home away from home.

"I had to make a decision. I thought you looked more like a boy than girl. They did the best they could. Things weren't so advanced back then. I still had your father's Army insurance, so we found a surgeon. They folded here, nipped this, tucked that, turned everything inside out. I don't know what the hell they did, but they made you into a boy."

"I suppose you thought it'd be funny, naming me John Thomas? Just to rub it in?"

"That wasn't my fault. I didn't know what it meant. Besides, it ain't like I named you Richard, is it? And it's better than some crazy gook name, ain't it?"

I had only one thing left to say: "Your husband is dead. Did you know that?"

"'Course I knew. They sent a letter years ago."

"Thanks for letting me know."

"What's the difference? He was dead before he died."

"But maybe Sun was alive for a while, before they sprayed her."

I slammed the phone. It should have shattered, but it didn't. I was impotent in every way.

"It ain't all bad," Rosie said. "You got some good luck with the bad."

"You're kidding, I hope?"

"I ain't kidding. Look."

She picked up a newspaper from the stack beside the couch.

"'Unclaimed ticket wins,'" she read. "You see that? And that's my birthday number. Ain't that the number you play? We gonna be rich, John. I promise, I won't even call you Uncle Tom no more. The good Lord came through like a motherfucker."

I tore off the page, folded and slipped it into the shirt pocket where I now kept my wallet.

"*We* won't be rich," I said. "But I will."

"What the fuck you talking about?"

"I'm leaving, Rosie. Leaving you, leaving everybody. You can have this cabin. You can have the fake wood paneling and the shag rug carpet and the piece of shit TV."

"Naw," she said. "You ain't going nowhere. I'll block the way. You won't get through me."

Finale

I started rolling toward the door until my dead thighs bumped her legs. And then I rolled right over her toes.

"You motherfucker."

She pitched over and fell on the floor. I pushed toward her. "Don't make me have to run you over. This thing's engineered to go up stairs. It can damn well handle you."

She flopped out of the way. I opened the door by running into it and kept rolling. I was halfway to the road before she made it to her feet and a quarter mile further when she lost her breath trying to catch me.

"Fucking nigger," she shouted. "Chink faggot!"

I kept rolling, but I wasn't wandering. I had a direction. It was a Giant Travel Plaza phone. On that phone, I would call the Lottery Commission, then collect my winnings the next day. And after that, I would call real estate agents and ask how they'd like to make a fast commission.

He was a nice man, that Century 21 fella, young and full of juice.

"You ever get lonely," I told him, "I got a list of girls you can call any time."

"Well," he said.

"Well, yes, here we are: Crack of all cracks."

"Huh?"

I shook my head. "Nothing. I'm so goddamned tired I think I'm sleeping on my feet."

He had the courtesy not to correct me.

Why? Why did they do it? I'll start with Rosie. The divorce proceedings allow my attorney to show me copies of her medical bills. Diagnosis: Schizoaffective. Whether the schiz affects her or she effects the schiz, who's to say? That *would* explain her so-called religion and those songs she sang. It explains a lot, but not everything.

And Mother? She thought Rosie would make a man of me at last, if

Rosie could only hold me down long enough, just like the doctors and nurses had done so many years before. Rosie was supposed to finished the job, stitch the mental halves together and smack me a second time. Then: "Here I am, one hundred percent male, with lawn mower and a passion for professional sports."

Mother had a dark thought that spread via word of mouth. Another prophet. Like them, she wrapped me in her fever dreams, the "we're-all-in-this-together" end of days. She planned it slow, step by step: "Now you're a believer, and don't forget your asbestos suit."

What about the funeral? That should be a once-in-lifetime event for everybody: Lovers' Day. They all come to your house. You laugh, cry, engage in nostalgic chatter, like a funeral, except you're still alive. The coffin was a joke meant to shake me with a spank: "Come to, Johnny boy. Welcome back to the world. Happy first birthday, again."

The telephone game, that's how it started, and every woman wheeled me closer to this chair. Each stop had its defining moment: The Very Worst of Jonathan Thomas, Volumes One through Eight, plus a bonus disk of B-sides, those women who don't even remember me, the crushes, the aborted one-night stands

What must it have been like to love a man who hated himself? I couldn't possibly know. I should have sent sympathy cards to everyone involved: "Sorry I'm dead. Wishing you comfort in your time of sorrow."

Yes, I sympathize now. I wonder if they knew the start of the story but could only guess the end, like a parable heard but only half-remembered. Still, half a parable is closer to the truth than the whole thing because it leaves you right where you started and doesn't pretend to take you anywhere better. How many mothers waiting for their prodigal sons? How many fathers smiling at the duplicate adventures of their offspring until it isn't funny anymore, just as they stop laughing around forty years of age, when the night before becomes

Finale

a tale they'll never tell themselves, much less brag to every friend in town? One day, they think, they'll divvy up the fatted calf. Sure they will.

Rosie, no thanks for the memories. Mary, good luck finding the 1920s. Azal, you might have been the one, if not for the murderousness between us. Kerrie, the law got in the way. Marnie, thanks for the moped. Chartrise, we came close to three. Caitlin, I'd send a wedding gift but, you know, I doubt the wedding's gonna happen. Holly, you go lightly. Daddy? We wouldn't have gotten along so well, probably. Mommy, who can blame you? Luckily, you both got out in time.

I bear no grudges, except one. Mother—"Mother"—sorry about the holes in the pantyhose. Funny, it all comes down to holes. I suggest you pretend the sun is going down all day long. Break your rule and have a morning drink. What the hell's the difference? I'm sure you've got the shakes. Did I say I forgive you? Hmm...

And me? I live in a new canyon house. The place is white and hums with ambient timelessness. The postman rings when delivering the mail. Too late now. Except for legal notices from attorneys, I never hear from anyone because there's no telephone. I cut that cord myself. What would I say?

Instead, I write, and I'm almost done. My words may seem to cling, but they remain in motion. If one looks closely, the hieroglyphs shimmy right off the page.

Now I've reached the end of destination and description, the twin motives of my existence. Nowhere to go, nothing to say.

My body no longer concerns me. It has no demands besides emptying. The painkillers help. They kill so much pain, I forget I'm alive. I go back to the locale that precedes birthplace. All the way back, in fact.

Look: Here come my last words.

What's it like to be unborn?

I have a dream that is not at all a dream. I inch outside my skin, like a caterpillar. Where I'm going, it will be very quiet.

The walls dissipate. I swim through milk. I head backwards, into the egg, and soon I will exit out the back door, to whatever lay beyond. I've been getting closer and closer. The moment is coming. Right now will do.

See? There's the last sunrise. Take a good look. I'm not anxious; soon, all nerves will be strudel.

Streams of sperm river-run the sky. Heads of gods bob past me. I kick them like soccer balls. I stick a pin in the devil's balloon. I'm going up, up and away. I see exactly what I was programmed to see but from the distance of my choosing. I see the first fires and a few mushroom clouds, and then it's gone, everything and everyone. I get out in the nick of time.

So sayonara to me, starshot and disappearing in the napalm dust. No more birthdays; no more funerals. My light may be visible, but I am long gone.

"Nakon, azizam," I tell myself whenever I look back. "Nakon, my baby boy."

About the Author

Paul A. Toth lives in Florida and, aside from his work as a novelist, writes short stories and poetry, a well as the occasional nonfiction piece. His short fiction and multimedia work have been widely published, with credits including *The Barcelona Review, Mississippi Review Online, Iowa Review,* and many others.

Printed in the United States
220749BV00001B/2/P

9 781933 293844